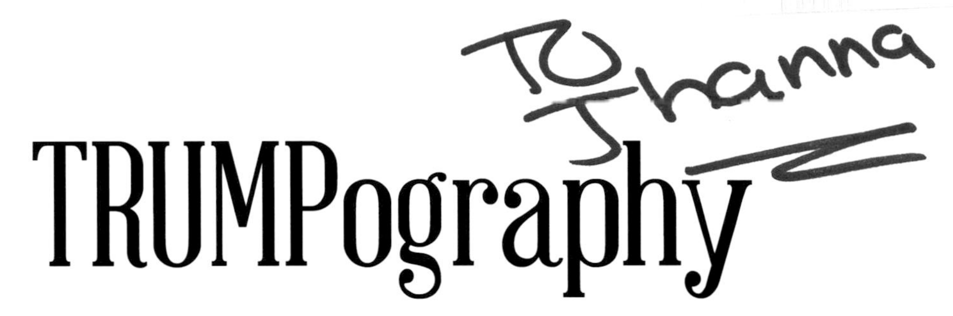

# TRUMPography

## How Biblical Principles Paved the Way to the American Presidency

Gene Ho

TRUMPography
HOW BIBLICAL PRINCIPLES PAVED THE WAY TO THE AMERICAN PRESIDENCY



iUniverse books may be ordered through booksellers or by contacting:

iUniverse
1663 Liberty Drive
Bloomington, IN 47403
www.iuniverse.com
1-800-Authors (1-800-288-4677)



ISBN: 978-1-5320-5138-8 (sc)
ISBN: 978-1-5320-5139-5 (e)

Library of Congress Control Number: 2018907438

Print information available on the last page.

iUniverse rev. date: 06/27/2018

# Table of Contents

# Acknowledgments

**Polen Ho**
For being the voice inside my head, pushing me always.

**Emily Massingill**
For your wordsmithery and patience.

**Gerald Bruehlman**
For courage & confidence.

**Arlene Jaskot**
For standing with me against the giant.

**Donald Trump**
For being the catalyst of conversation.

**Nadean Ho**
For being my best friend, my true north, my Esther.

One of the most exciting thrills for me during the campaign was to see where my photos would eventually turn up.
For my part: I would take pictures at an event and then submit them to the team...

I would stumble across my images in the most exciting, and sometimes unexpected places. One of my images wrapped the Trump bus. Others found their way to news articles. Sometimes they were featured in Tweets, and in other times they were used in campaign ads.

I was grateful for the opportunity to share my eye.

# Introduction

This all started with a wish,
a product of opportunities
after putting myself in the position to receive them.
But things don't always work out like you plan.
Perhaps that's because—sometimes—the plan is much bigger than you are.

After two years of following the man who would become
the president of the United States of America
on his homegrown campaign,
my wish was to become the White House photographer.

As a small-business owner and father of four, I prepared myself
for the real possibility of what might lie ahead when
I submitted my résumé and awaited the call.

That call never came.

What followed was the worst year of my life.
Between a frivolous lawsuit and a yearlong IRS tax audit,
I was brought to my knees.
It was only then, in the darkness, that things started to become clear.
I awoke.
A lucidity washed over me;
the frantic panic and fear of the year gone by started to make sense.

My legs had been broken.
My spirit stalled.
And in that time, He carried me.
[Psalm 23]

As I sat and unraveled the map of my trodden path, it became clear why I wasn't offered the position as White House photographer.
There was something else I was called to do,
and it led me here to you.

----

Remember yourself as a child,
collecting dandelion wishes …
The seeds started as a beautiful, delicate orb in your still-perfect hands.
Pouring breath from your lungs, you'd blow.
The seeds would scatter to the wind, floating to their places on the earth.
You believed, the unpolluted innocence of a child.
With faith unshaken,
those tiny seeds would carry your wish to become true.

- Still other seed fell on good soil where it produced a crop …
He who has ears, let him hear.
—Matthew 13:8–9

****

With the faith of His child, my wish is no longer for me but for *all of us.*

I hope you may consider this book a pocket full of seeds,
an opportunity.
Let's talk again. Let's pray again. Let's believe again.

I call this photo "A Billionaire Starts His Day."
This picture was taken on the first day I worked for Trump.

This photo became a metaphor for the adventure that followed:
He started from the ground and worked his way to the top.

Trump travelled to this event on his own private jet to speak to a group of business owners.
The room held about 50 or so entrepreneurs.

I wonder how many friends think they are bluffing, when those few in attendance say
they sat in on a Donald Trump speech with enough room to stretch their legs.

You have to start something, in order to finish it.
****
He started by believing he could.

A personal favorite photo from the campaign trail
that, to my knowledge, was never used
in any of the campaign promotions.

I've since asked individuals outside the campaign their opinion on this image.

Some felt that perhaps Trump looked too "Hollywood" in this picture.
Early in the campaign, there were people who would approach Trump with
references to "The Apprentice" days by giving a classic, "You're Fired!"

Midway through the campaign, Trump pivoted from being the television-star to a powerhouse candidate.

I had hoped that this photo could have used by the campaign,
but I can see it being a bit more suited for the jovial celebrity Trump than the President Trump.

Part of what I did was work to capture the different aspects of Trump;
covering the solemn as well as the lighthearted side of his personality.

# Chapter 1

## Absalom—The Humble Charmer

"Look, your claims are valid and proper, but there is no representative of the king to hear you." And Absalom would add, "If only I were appointed judge in the land! Then everyone who has a complaint or case could come to me and I would see that they receive justice."

Also, whenever anyone approached him to bow down before him, Absalom would reach out his hand, take hold of him and kiss him. Absalom behaved in this way toward all the Israelites who came to the king asking for justice, and so he stole the hearts of the people of Israel.

—2 Samuel 15:3–6

January 19, 2015—A door opened; I walked through. This day began a two-year adventure that put miles on my car and revolutions on my camera's shutter count. This was my inaugural date as campaign photographer for the man who would become the president of the United States of America.

I never could have known the road that lay ahead and how it would forever change my life. We, the people, had no idea the gravity of our situation. We, the voting people, never could have imagined the pushback we would receive for supporting a candidate who didn't fall in line with the status quo.

Donald Trump wasn't always the easiest boss to work for. Mr. Trump wasn't always the easiest candidate to love. Mr. Donald J. Trump is a man. He is riddled with flaws, capable of sin and regret. Still he lives with great bravery. All the same can be said for the first man, Adam. As can be said for Moses. As can be said for King David. As can be said for you.

I took a detour from my regular life to chase this campaign. I was exhausted, overwhelmed, and sometimes out of my element. When it was all said and done, my parting gift from presidential politics was somewhat ironic, I suppose:

A faith renewed.

What follows is in part personal experiences and memories, another part biblical truth that I felt paralleled the underlying biblical principles:

A foot in the sea, a foot on land.

****

In my time on the 2015–16 campaign trail, I had the unique privilege of taking photos of Mr. Donald J. Trump. One could certainly argue there were more qualified photojournalists available. However, I don't believe it was an accident that a seasoned wedding photographer happened into the position. More on that later.

I wiggled my way into a front-row seat early on and grabbed my popcorn as the show began. Mr. Trump has never been one to disappoint his audiences, and the first days (long before he'd declared his candidacy) were no different. Since I wasn't shooting these events with the classic newsprint objective, my signature wide-angle fish-eye shots became a unique staple in the Trump marketing engine. However, I spent most of my time with Mr. Trump behind the scenes in the "click line," which was my primary duty.

The click line is where someone of noted importance stands in place, often in front of a backdrop. Then, for the sake of efficiency, a line is formed, and each person in that line takes a turn for a photo alongside the guest of honor. Most of the time, it's a celebrity, a politician, or, if you're at Disney, Elsa. It's more commonly referred to as a VIP meet and greet. But it's also known as the grip and grin—as the line travels through, the person of the hour will grip for a handshake and grin for the camera.

This was one of the most rewarding and insightful experiences I had on the campaign. Since the process was long, it was also where I formed some of the closest bonds. I routinely arrived several hours in advance to scout the location and get my bearings. Upon arrival, I would size up the room designated for the meet and greet. I set out to overcome the changeable challenges while mentally preparing myself for those beyond my control.

Traditional setup included a plain black backdrop. Sometimes it was as basic as a solid wall or curtain. Later, as it became obvious that Mr. Trump was throwing his red 'Make America Great Again' hat in the ring, two flags were added. One flag was, of course, Old Glory, the faithful red, white, and blue. The second flag was the flag for that particular state.

From a photographer's standpoint, the lighting was usually nothing short of a nightmare. Many of the places where we were sequestered were tiny boardrooms or conference center meeting rooms. However, the back rooms and out-of-the-way locations were suitable since the click line was private.

Those fortunate enough to land a spot in the meet and greet line would often show up hours before Mr. Trump was even sharing the state's airspace. One of the most interesting studies for me was people watching those lucky chosen ones. It became a pastime for me to imagine what had brought them to be in the room in the first place. More interesting still was to wonder how vocal their support for the Trump train was in their regular lives.

While I've done photos of Mr. Trump with guests at high-dollar dinners, those events were few and far between. The ritzy fundraising gigs commissioned for the Republican National Committee came late in the game. It was not something Trump had created for himself.

The truth is the people I saw in Donald Trump's VIP meet and greet lines were, by and far, us "regular" people.

On occasion there was a local politician, of sorts, in attendance. It was typically a state senator or US representative. There were times when members of Trump's extended family were there as VIP members. Sometimes there were regionally relevant celebrity endorsements.

However, the vast majority of the meet and greets were made up of ordinary, everyday, hardworking Americans. There were campaign volunteers and the family members of staff. Some were people who'd offered office space to the locally run campaign offices. Some were individuals who had simply opened their homes to debate watch parties. Most typical VIP lines are made of money, but for Mr. Trump it didn't seem to be an honor bestowed only on those who could afford it. Rather it was given to those who deserved it. To prove that further was the group Trump always had time for: the first responders and veterans. These were men and women from the fire departments, local police, highway patrol, and their dispatchers, along with the brave men and women who had made sacrifices and contributed to the US military.

Trump insisted on these photos and delighted in showing his appreciation for their time and their heart. Before me stood action, not words.

These gatherings were filled with well-deserving, unassuming, hardworking patriots. Most often that's who I saw run through those lines to meet the Republican candidate. It was a beautiful testimony to the Trump staff. They were given the liberty to determine who would have access, and they sent the invitations. If there was a highlight to the grassroots campaign, I can tell you that it was done effectively by way of the meet and greet experience.

If there was one resounding commonality throughout, the campaign was never about who had the most money or who could buy influence. It was about those who demanded change and stood for it. It was about those who followed faithfully, believing he could be the catalyst to bring that change.

The meet and greets were a way of life for me on the campaign trail. They were where the rubber met the road, where our presidential candidate came face-to-face with those he desired to represent. Through meet and greets, I was able to witness firsthand the man we were told America loved to hate.

**Meet Absalom**

Absalom, the son of King David, was known for his cutthroat schemes and relentless drive to overtake the kingdom from his father. At the same time, he was well known for his smooth talking and striking physical beauty. In fact, it was said that there was not a man in all the land so highly praised for his handsome appearance. Specifically, he was recognized for his Pantene-advertisement-worthy hair.

> Whenever he cut the hair of his head … he would weigh
> it, and its weight was two hundred shekels.
> —2 Samuel 14:26

That translates to five pounds. To be honest, I don't know that most of us will grow five pounds of hair in our lifetimes, but Absalom was clearly an overachiever in this department. Some three thousand years ago, and we're still talking about those Guinness Book locks.

King David had many sons, nineteen mentioned by name in the Bible. Absalom was the third born. Through Absalom's lifetime there was much unrest among the sons of David; many of the upheavals involved Absalom in some way. The battles among David's heirs to the throne involved rape, murder, and much rebellion. Power struggle and revenge run deep throughout history, and mighty David's household was no exception to the rule.

Amnon was the first son of David and held the birthright as heir to the throne. In a sin that proved fateful, Amnon lusted after his half sister, Tamar. He eventually raped and abandoned her. As her full-blooded sibling, Absalom vowed justice would be served. For two years, he never spoke a word of it to Amnon but awaited an opportunity to exact his revenge. In the presence of their brothers, he orchestrated a party and publicly ordered Amnon's murder.

In some places, the Bible is the original *The Art of War*, and history was not whitewashed. Brutal as it may be, this is our past. What is left for us to do is learn from what we read and attempt to apply those lessons for our own betterment. Many of the uprisings during David's reign could have been contained if, as a father, David had been more disciplinarian. However, after years of inaction from his father, Absalom sought to rectify the situation.

After the murder of his half brother Amnon, Absalom fled and found refuge in a neighboring kingdom. After three years, King David and Absalom reconciled, and Absalom returned home. Still Absalom's contempt for his father continued to fester, and more than ever before, he aspired to take over the kingship.

Absalom was a devilish charmer. But to become king wasn't always as simple as being next on the list. His position was made difficult with nearly twenty brothers contending for the spot. It was made even more challenging because he'd fallen out of Dad's good graces after killing one of them. Absalom devised a long-term strategy. He would launch his ploy by first setting out to win the hearts of the people.

To do this, he began by creating a spectacular entourage. With a magnificent chariot, horses, and fifty men running ahead of him, he stationed himself at the city gates. When the villagers passed, seeking to bring issues before the king, Absalom would step in to lend his ear. Compassionate and patient, and oh so dreamy, he would listen to them.

He pledged that if only he were king, he would have the authority to administer justice for them. As you can imagine, because he was the king's son, when people approached him, they would immediately bow down to him. When that happened, Absalom would counter. Rather than let people bow, he would rush in to stop them, humbly helping them to their feet.

While he did so, he would reach in and kiss their hands. It sent this message to those "less" than he: "Yes, I am the king's son, but we are one and the same seeking a greater kingdom. What's more, I am here to serve you." You can only imagine how smitten the kingdom's people must have been. The son of the king! Like some Bronze Age Fabio. Surely they were starstruck. It was dramatically effective in winning hearts, and understandably so.

The concept isn't so foreign to us now. Through the years, plenty of politicians have employed similar techniques—the roll-up-your-sleeves, regular Joe approach. If it were only that simple, we would all be kings. But Absalom's technique, whether contrived or sincere, worked because he was already famous.

Average people can try this method. While they may win over a few, they also run the risk of taking a few shots to the nose. Today's results wouldn't nearly match up. Absalom won over an entire kingdom, one at a time—person-to-person with simple, submissive humility and the patience to listen.

Before meeting him, people of the time must have thought of Absalom as a vain son of the king, a silver spoon murderer. That is precisely why it worked for him. There was a predetermined idea about the type of man he would be.

We, like Absalom, and we, like Trump, work to create a character that fairly represents us. We seek to build a reputation that precedes us. But sometimes the *idea* of who we are takes on a life of its own. For good or bad, we are judged in the eyes of our peers. We become simply the plumber, the smoker, the mom, or the lawyer, but we aren't merely one thing. We cross over and encompass so much more than the titles we are most known for. As individuals, the greatest gift and challenge we have is the ability to see the best in people.

Anyone can see the dirt in someone. Be the one who finds the gold.

**Enter Trump**

It was November 2015; I had been taking pictures of the Trump following for eleven months, and we were settled into a routine and workflow. Prior to this point, Trump didn't have United States Secret Service protection. He had been using his own private security team. This month things changed.

For nearly a year, I had managed the click line. Through the early days of the campaign, I occasionally suggested individuals to receive invitations to meet Trump. By managing, I don't mean that I had full authority to dictate who was in the line. When I say I controlled the line, specifically I told people where to form the line, where it began and ended, and when to join us for their photo. Before the Secret Service, the functional aspects of the click line were my domain. I controlled it. When Secret Service was implemented, that changed.

With Secret Service protection, there was a new sheriff in town, and it came with authority. The first meet and greet line brought an immediate change that begged notice. To begin with, the number of people invited backstage was virtually cut in half. The event became considerably more structured with a more polished feel. I no longer called the shots as far as where Trump would station himself and how the click line would function. I didn't mind losing this control. Besides the fact that it was less work and preparation for me, the men in black were dealt considerably more respect than I amassed with a camera.

One of the biggest changes to the overall campaign included Trump's longtime personal bodyguard, Keith Schiller. When the Secret Service stepped in, Keith was no longer our little family's hub of security. By now, most of the Trump campaign staff had gotten used to Mr. Schiller calling the shots. Keith is probably six foot six, a physically intimidating stature. He could have gotten all the respect he needed with his size alone. Keith's personality, however, is exactly the opposite of his monstrous exterior. He is the classic gentle giant. He earned respect not for a stern fist, but for his invested heart. A simple nod in the right direction was enough to have us moving.

After Secret Service took over, Keith stayed at Trump's side, but he was no longer head of overall security. It was my understanding at that time that Keith was asked to surrender his firearm. He remained, unarmed, at the forefront, a testament to his loyalty to Mr. Trump. With or without it, there was no doubt at any time that it was Keith who had Trump's back.

Overall we loved the new changes in large part because, ultimately, it legitimized everything we were doing. Once assigned Secret Service detail, there was a decided difference. We'd gone from a campaign supporting a candidate to a campaign supporting a candidate requiring third-party protection assigned by the United States government. In short, it was now legitimately presidential.

In November 2015, the Secret Service entered. Let me share the situation on that first day of newly established full-coverage security. The buzz was undeniable. Not only was the staff aware that Trump now had Secret Service, but so was everyone else in attendance. Those backstage felt significant—I dare say superior. They had been screened quite heavily to be allowed to attend. There was an ever-growing sense of how momentous this was. There was an historical appreciation and understanding that to look around you meant seeing future history books. Everyone was excited because they were about to meet their candidate, Mr. Donald J. Trump, our official, heavily protected, legitimate, future president. In so many ways the added security coverage felt like a victory. It felt as if Trump had already won.

The room took on an eerie calm when one of the staffers reported that Trump's plane was ten minutes out. I was used to that warning. Before this day, I was the one who asked for the ETA, and I was the one who broadcast it to the eager masses. But again, things were different now.

As soon as the staffer reported this, just loudly enough for listening ears to hear, everyone fell into place as though casual citizens were now ready at attention.

In the history of my career as a photographer, this makes the short list of my proudest memories: In prior months Trump had walked into the room with a loosely formed line, with minimal structure and a somewhat chaotic welcome. But, as I said, *this* time was different. With Secret Service in control of the heavy lifting, I had a perfectly formed, reverent line beside me. For the next five minutes, as we anticipated our candidate's arrival, we stood there, hushed.

The expression of gratitude on Mr. Trump's face when he walked into the room said all it needed to. He saw how different things were on this day, and it was just as special for him. He walked into the room with his photographer standing at attention, heading a respectfully formed, well-prepared line. Rarely had there been an opportunity to greet me formally at these VIP events with the fast pace we'd gotten used to, hitting the ground running. I will never forget this time. With a look of authentic appreciation, he shook his fist, pointed my way, and said, "There's my man!"

"We're ready for you, Mr. Trump," I said.

There we were, off and running. Again. Still reminiscent of a first time.

The first in line joined Mr. Trump in front of the set, and I started clicking frames at breakneck pace. This was the name of the game for me. I had an interesting position. My primary objective was to get a photograph of Mr. Trump with everyone in that line, with an interesting caveat: I had to get it done with a speed level that left me in the boss's favor *and* winning with the masses.

Barring conversation, getting through a line of thirty people would normally take me less than ten minutes. I would brief my VIPs beforehand to inform them whether Mr. Trump had time for autographs and insist we keep conversations to a minimum when the schedule was tight, but the idea of "barring conversation" was not remotely possible. Not only was Mr. Trump a candidate running for president, but he was also an established celebrity. One of the toughest hurdles as his photographer was keeping the line efficiently moving.

Understandably, those lucky enough to land a spot in that line wanted to have a moment with Mr. Trump to share a personal story, ask for an autograph, or discuss their issues. My reserved and orderly little lineup of VIPs had been attentive and applauded as Trump walked into the room, but even with Secret Service, as the click line started moving along, my tried-and-true performance again became necessary. After the picture was taken, I had to step in as the responsible party and break up the long-awaited moment with our future president.

He and I had played this exchange before. With the time constraints on this day, it was my job to "bully" my way in and act as the authority to end the conversation. It was imperative that the line kept moving to maintain the schedule for his slated stage time. On this day, this day of a newly established higher power, Trump's reaction to my routine was telling of the man he is.

Rather than taking my out and feigning to reluctantly end the conversation, he held out his hand to me as if to say stop. Without having missed a beat of the conversation, Trump continued intently listening, giving time that those of us organizing his schedule knew he didn't have.

On this day, his actions reminded me of Absalom.

Absalom carried himself as stately, yet approachable. The efficacy of Absalom's charm is that those around him began to view him as the one in power and would bow down to him as king. Humbly, he pulled them to their feet, insisting he was not worthy—just as Trump sacrificed his time and offered it to hear his supporters' concerns.

Trump stole hearts. He stole the hearts of the American people by simply making time for them. It was a way to express to his supporters that they were more important than anything he had going on at the time. He made it clear in action: your opinion and your thoughts or your troubles are valid. When they finally had that moment with Mr. Trump, he pushed away the clock and gave them his full attention.

****

I saw the same principle play out just a few weeks later. We were in the belly of a convention center. It was unique in the sense that normally we were in a relatively small room, but on this day, it was quite a large space. On his arrival you could clearly see him enter the large room from the far end and walk the length of the room toward us. While we could see him coming, he could also see who was in our crowd as he approached.

On this day, waiting for Mr. Trump was none other than "the king": NASCAR legend Richard Petty. In his signature cowboy hat, trademark sunglasses, and a smile that wouldn't quit, there was no way you could miss that it was Richard Petty.

Trump knew Petty was there. We knew Petty was there. Everyone in that room was fumbling to process being in the same room with both Donald Trump and Richard Petty—*at the same time!*

Just as Absalom reached out his hand, so did Trump. But it wasn't first to Petty. After that long walk to join us, the first hands he reached to acknowledge were those of our first responders.

Imagine that. Trump walked into the room, and the person he greeted first—the person he reached out his hand to—was not the celebrity everyone had been whispering about but the officer of the law. This, in action, was the charm of Trump.

In the beginning, before Secret Service and before he won the Republican nomination, it was as if Trump had envisioned himself as president. He chose to carry himself as such and bore the responsibility of the position he hadn't yet been given.

In the campaign's infancy, the meet and greet sessions were more like a private cocktail hour—minus the cocktails, of course. Sometimes there was an air of organized formality. But many times, it was just Trump and America in a room socializing.

During one of these events, a woman approached Mr. Trump with an issue. She was pleading for help as if he were already holding the office he sought. After a short, intense discussion, Trump paused and said, "Hold on …" He looked over her not-so-tall stature and scanned the room. Then he shouted, "Hope!" as he waved over one of his chief confidants, spokesperson Hope Hicks.

"Hope, can we get more information and take care of this?" Trump asked.

Mr. Trump wasn't president yet, but very much like Absalom, he was prepared to find the proper channels in order to provide as much assistance as he was able. If there was something he could do then and now, even merely as a fellow human being, he would go out of his way to find the avenues to do it.

Motives are invisible, but they are the true test of character.
—Alfred A Montapert

One of the last great days before things changed.
Trump loved to walk down the center aisle before he gave a talk, shaking hands as he approached the stage.
This picture was taken while Trump still had his personal security team.
This team was the best of the best; many of them former NYPD.

This private security team allowed Trump to walk down the middle of
the venue and I was allowed to stand at the front of the room as he took the stage.
He had a rock star presence walking through the crowds.
This practice came to an end when Secret Service took over security.

Later the same day, as Trump left
the venue. The crowds would
follow him to
his private motorcade.

After Secret Service controlled things,
Trump left from more secure,
undisclosed locations.

The first campaign talks were given
to rooms of 50-100 in attendance.
Whether Trump held the attention of 2 or 20,000,
he carried the same passion for his message.

Top: Talk given to the
State Financial Officers Foundation.
Carly Fiorina also spoke at this event and
had "stronger billing"
- meaning she spoke later that day,
in the "preferred" time slot.

Above, Right: Trump speaking to Charleston area business leaders.
On this day Trump flew his jet from New York to Charleston, SC
to speak to a total head count of 200, at best.

****

Even great things start small.

# Chapter 2

### Jonah—The Reluctant Messenger

The word of the Lord came to Jonah, son of Amittai: "Go to the great city of Nineveh and preach against it, because its wickedness has come up before me." But Jonah ran away from the Lord and headed for Tarshish. He went down to Joppa, where he found a ship bound for that port. After paying the fare, he went aboard and sailed for Tarshish to flee from the Lord.

—Jonah 1:1–3

Have you ever felt moved to do something you wouldn't normally do? Something so unusual that your closest friends and family question you, perhaps not for what it is but for how out of character it might seem for you?

At the age of eighteen, fresh out of high school, I ventured southward on the East Coast and transplanted myself from Long Island, New York, to Myrtle Beach, South Carolina, to attend college. That in itself isn't earth-shattering. People do this every day; it's nothing special to pick up everything and move.

After the first few months in Myrtle Beach, I decided this beautifully booming melting pot of misfits felt like it fit, and I decided to stay. This wasn't any kind of historic, biblically inspired move. Even though it wasn't something I had previously considered, the forks in the road led me there, and it felt like home … It felt like promise … It felt like it was mine.

I didn't have any family in Myrtle Beach. I didn't have a girlfriend. Frankly, I didn't even have a plan at the time, but something made me feel like I belonged. In retrospect, it was one of the best decisions I've ever made.

Again, it's not some milestone that changes the landscape of history. But it forever shaped what would become *my* history.

My wife, Nadean, (some years later) also elected to pick up and move. At eighteen, she packed her Honda Del-Sol, and with a dart on an atlas, she left the Holsteins in Wisconsin and rode eleven hundred miles to Myrtle Beach.

Perhaps it was fate or coincidence that we found one another. Like homing pigeons charting out a course to find the future home we would share together, I believe we simply followed the map. One thing is clear: none of the personal accounts you've read this far would be possible without both of us being willing to take that initial risk to come to where we are.

Luck does not come around often. So when it does, be sure to take
full advantage of it, even if it means working very hard.
—Donald Trump

All those decisions seemed on a whim—the bumps, the hurt, and all the times I took the long way home. All roads eventually led me down a path that crossed the path of Donald Trump. It brought me to a place where I was led to consider how his choices were just as poetically timed. I was left to wonder whether the decision to run for president was an action he chose or a reaction to his perceived absence of a suitable candidate. I believe he felt compelled to act, not because it was something he wanted to do, but because he was being led to at the hand of God—whether he knew it or not.

The general public views Donald Trump's larger-than-life story from the outside as though things have come easy. "He was given a million dollars by his dad," they say. "He didn't do it himself; it was handed to him," they add. I mean absolutely no disrespect when I say this, but he has siblings who *also* would have been given a million dollars to blaze into the world with. It seems a fair note to mention that they are not also household names.

From the outside, it would appear he simply decides to do something, and it happens. I can report firsthand that this is the furthest from the truth. Donald Trump is much like any of us. He just swings the bat far more often than the rest of us do. Half the battle is having the kind of confidence that's unshaken by failures. Just like DJT, we weigh the decision and debate the pros and cons. We consider how it could potentially affect our family and those around us. We calculate the odds for success; we consider the costs. After putting all the necessary heart and head to work, we get to the grind (or we've talked ourselves out of it). Once the commitment is made, we *do*—with reckless abandon. Nothing will stop the will to succeed as long as one has the will to succeed.

Just because the goal had been set doesn't mean it didn't come with critics, doubters, and people who wanted to see him fail. In many ways, I believe Trump is much like Jonah in that he questioned what he felt led to do. Having witnessed Trump's following from day one, I can tell you the campaign wasn't always exceeding the wildest imaginations. Things didn't *start* as rallies with ten thousand people and a live Facebook feed. This movement instead started small, just a tiny spark. Trump would move to the front of a room, speaking to a mere fifty starstruck Americans, discussing relatively general concepts on how America could improve. The occasional patron would yell, "When are you going to run?" To which he would shake his head, "No, no, it's not for me."

There had to have been days very early on when Trump must have questioned what on earth he was doing. I would love to see a cost analysis on that early campaign. On his own personal dime, day after day, he fueled up his personal jet—taking time out of his "real job" and leaving his family—to run around the countryside and hold speaking arrangements, all for a room of fifty supporters. Whether or not he felt it could be enough to have an impact at all, he carried on.

As the months carried forward, I began to see that same small spark building heat. At an event, probably close to a year after the campaign began, I overheard Trump whisper to his event coordinator, "Can you believe this is happening?"

Even in the campaign's infancy, most of the regulars involved truly believed things would play out as they have. Through the bumps in the road, I too kept the faith. I witnessed the first talks to those small crowds and the way Trump resonated with people. I watched him hone in on talking points, and I was there when the numbers began to grow. Friends, neighbors, and colleagues would inquire in hushed voices. As the sparks grew into a fire, I knew how many were standing in the silent majority. I had a front-row seat and watched that once tiny spark ignite to become an unstoppable wildfire.

While Donald Trump is a man well versed in scrutiny, early on the media had taken an unmistakable interest in blasting him each time he spoke. My wife would say, "Nothing truly great comes without stepping out of the comfort zone." In other words, be bold enough to take the risk, stay strong in your convictions, and expect it to be difficult. After all, if it were easy, everyone would be doing it. However, the verbal ridicule against Trump was relentless. You wonder if Trump, especially early on, questioned why he was continuing to stick his neck out when the backlash was so intense.

We can only speculate what Mr. Trump's goals were from the beginning. I was deadlocked on mine from the first day out. My objective was to see that first day carry all the way to the last day of the campaign. And it goes without saying, we wanted a victory, but there were more than a few monkey wrenches along the way. The biggest hurdle surrounded my first boss, Corey Lewandowski. Just before Trump won the Republican nomination, Lewandowski, his campaign manager, was let go.

I had known and worked with him for close to a year and a half, and by then the organization had grown quite large. It was routine and straightforward to be able to report directly to Lewandowski. Things were effective while he was in command. I could always fall back on the line, "Well, Corey said …" Of course, I didn't always use that card. I made sure to use that appeal to a higher authority at a minimum.

Mr. Trump didn't use emails as a means of communication, but Lewandowski as our point of contact did. Initially I was quite intimidated by Corey. His emails and correspondence were always effective albeit terse. I would rattle on in a long email detailing a particular day, and he would answer with a simple yes or no. I once asked his advice on how to proceed with the media's request for an interview, and he answered with a concise "Pass." There was peace in knowing Mr. Trump trusted Corey's guidance. Corey felt like a secure handle and a fast ear to the man on top. I had really grown to appreciate having him, and we became friends in the chaos of the campaign. We found a common bond: we are both older dads, and our sons are close in age. The day he met my son, the usual businesslike tightness left his jaw, and his eyes softened so you could see the father in him. We were able to grow together on a common thread, knowing our sons while now so young were unable to grasp the magnitude of the work we were doing.

Near the end of his time with the campaign, I felt things were going my way. If I needed something or if I had a question, I would email Lewandowski directly and almost instantly have a straight answer. However, this all came to a crashing halt on June 20, 2016, when we learned Lewandowski was no longer our campaign manager.

The lights went out when he was let go from the campaign.

The first day without Corey was the hardest. At the first Trump rally after his departure, I had never felt so out of place in my life. I showed up to an event ready to do my job as usual. I was backstage, ready. I was there not because I had been instructed to be, but because it was routine up until this point, and no one had told me otherwise. I felt completely lost. I was a Lewandowski loyalist—and now he was gone. I wondered if I would be sidelined with him as well. Was I fired?

This was the most difficult period of the two years that I was amid the campaign. This was mere weeks before the Republican National Convention in Cleveland. I had always planned to be there. In this time of uncertainty, I didn't attend. I didn't know if I was still welcome. In the transition to our new campaign manager, there was radio silence.

I knew what it was like to feel out of place. I wonder how many times Trump might have felt like that during the campaign. He was out of the well-known wheelhouse of his building mogul routine, subjecting every aspect of himself to the media wolves. There was nothing too sacred to involve his business, his wife, and his young son. When he came to terms with the idea that he was going to have to take up for America and run for president, I imagine he must have sat quietly asking, "And you're *sure* we've got no one else?"

**Meet Jonah**

Jonah was a prophet, which means he was regarded as an inspired teacher or proclaimer of the will of God. While Jonah is one of the shortest books in the Bible, his story is most known to anyone with even a casual biblical knowledge. His story is best remembered because it's epic! He was swallowed by a whale—and lived.

Part of the intrigue and excitement with Jonah's story is that it seems to be the one critics talk about most, attempting to discredit the Bible. How could a man have been swallowed by a fish and live to tell the tale? Crazier things …

I present to you: Vesna Vulović, a Serbian flight attendant who is a Guinness Book of World Records holder. In 1972, Vesna fell 33,330 feet following an explosion on an airplane. She lived the remaining forty-four years of her life with a limp.

I could find one hundred more outrageous stories, but you see my point. If you were to play a game of "What would you rather," Jonah's story seems the more likely winner. Would you rather be blown up in a plane and fall over six miles to the ground with no parachute, or be regurgitated by a whale? Fish puke for me, please.

The difference is Vesna's story is easy to believe because you can track newspaper articles, DuckDuckGo the address of the hospital she was admitted to, or interview the man who found her alive in the field following her fall. For eighth century BC, we've just got to have faith that one of our ancestors penned Jonah's account accurately.

Ultimately, the lesson in Jonah's story boils down to a man who was scared. His father asked him to do something he didn't want to do. So he ran away.

Sometimes the stories seem so distant and the players so great, we forget this is history. God used and *is using* real, live people—oftentimes unlikely candidates. The truth is if you study the lessons and emulate God's principles, the results will bode well for you and for your family. God only asks that we do our best. Mark Burns, a dear friend and Donald Trump's personal spiritual adviser, reminds us, "The qualifications for God's love are so little; simply believe."

The most striking piece of Jonah's story is that he was asked to do something by God Himself. He felt obligated to do something, and yet there was a profound struggle; he was dumbfounded and utterly fear-stricken.

This order was given to Jonah:

> Go to the great city of Nineveh and preach against it,
> because its wickedness has come up before me.
> —Jonah 1:2

This was Jonah's reaction:

> But Jonah ran away from the Lord and headed for Tarshish. He went down to Joppa, where he found a ship bound for that port. After paying the fare, he went aboard and sailed for Tarshish to flee from the Lord.
> —Jonah 1:3

At the time he was given instruction, Jonah was in a city called Joppa. God asked him to preach to the people of Ninevah. A trip to Ninevah for him would have been about five hundred miles, by land, to the east. Instead, Jonah got on a boat and set out in exactly the *opposite* direction, about twenty-five hundred miles to the west.

Imagine this in today's terms. Forget that it meant preaching to a savage enemy. Imagine it was routine work. You are in Columbus, Ohio, and your boss asks you to go to Philadelphia to deliver some pink slips. You *really* don't want to go. You're worried about the backlash, afraid that some of the recipients of the termination notice may take it out on you personally. So instead, you get in your car and drive twenty-five hundred miles in the opposite direction to San Francisco, California. That is the distance we're talking about here.

Jonah didn't even entertain the idea. He was running as fast as the ocean would take him—and almost as far as he could physically go—as if he was removing himself completely from a potential reissue of the request. He was gone as if he put a sign on the office door: "Jonah out to lunch. Forever."

This humanizes Jonah. Ultimately, this is an act of human nature. We've all had times in life when we felt like tossing up our hands and walking away from everything, the challenge seemingly insurmountable.

I don't believe Jonah was afraid to make a pronouncement. After all, Jonah was a prophet; he was used to preaching to the masses. The difference, this time, was that he was asked to speak in front of the people of Nineveh, the capital of Assyria. The Assyrian people of that time were known for their violence and brutality. It was, in fact, part of their national agenda. They learned that the more vulgarity they were known for, the more feared they would be by their neighbors. It was far better negotiating with the Assyrians because you didn't want to fight them in war.

Torture of their enemies was normal. Enemy soldiers were massacred; enemy kings were beheaded. Jonah was being asked to preach to these people to tell them that *his* God (not the Assyrian gods but Jonah's God) disapproved of them. Jonah was so fearful of the proposition that he would have rather died than carry out what he'd been asked to do. In his attempt to flee, the waters raged against his ship and he begged the crew:

> Pick me up and throw me into the sea …
> —Jonah 1:12

While near to death, in reflection and faith, Jonah had a change of heart and came to know (again) that with God all things are possible:

When my life was ebbing away, I remembered you … what I have vowed I will make good.
—Jonah 2:7–9

Sometimes in life we encounter challenges that seem so much greater than we are. We become paralyzed to act, facing the enormity of the task at hand. Often we can be our own biggest roadblock. While we know prolonging actions to resolve the problem will achieve nothing, we stand immobilized by fear. Or worse, we retreat to avoid the undertaking altogether. Inaction is a concerted effort. Rather than staring at the big picture, fearing the dozens of "what-if" results, break down measures into what can be done *now*. Plan. Organize. Believe. Act. All is for naught without the *act*.

My wife's grandfather was diagnosed with polio in the 1930s. While in the iron lung, at age six, he was told that *if* he survived, he would never walk again. Not only did he walk, but he also went on to raise five children. What's more, he did it while engaged in one of the toughest professions out there: farming. Today, at eighty-eight, he'll tell you this:

If it's tough—we'll get it done.
If it's impossible? It's just going to take a little longer.
—John Bruehlman

For better or worse, there are times in our lives when we wonder why in the world we are doing something. The answer can be so basic it's overlooked: because it's the right thing to do.

I have felt something driving me to write this book. The intent stems from a place of positivity and hope. It is not an endeavor I considered leading up to this point, but the words have come easily. Its purpose is not to convince recruits to faith, though that's a welcome bonus. My hope is to wake the weary, for us to be excited again to open the Bible and learn something about ourselves. Through writing this book and pouring through the pages of my own Bible, I realized that while I hadn't been running away from God, I wasn't running toward Him either.

Sometimes we don't know why we're compelled to do something. Then, when we least expect to find the answers, it makes perfect sense.

## Enter Trump

Everyone wants to know what it's like to be a rock star—if only for a second. For most of us, the closest we're going to get is belting out a power ballad on a major highway. I've always enjoyed living vicariously through others. Whenever I've had the chance, I've been known to dip my toes in the water just to see what it's like to bask in the glory of the limelight. A few years ago, I photographed a country rock concert with a massive crowd of over thirty thousand in attendance. They certainly hadn't come to see me, but the energy was insane! Before the headliner rose to take the mic, I took the opportunity to photograph the adoring fans from center stage. While there, I stopped to soak it up, and I pumped my fist to the crowd. The response was electrifying. To hear so many voices roaring in front of you is indescribable.

I've had my chance to do this at Trump rallies as well. Every once in a while, before Trump was in the building, I would take the stage to photograph the view from his podium. Trump's supporters waited for hours, staring at an empty stage and listening to Lee Greenwood's "God Bless the USA." Suddenly there I was: a photographer on stage to take their picture from Trump's vantage point. The people went crazy. When I did have the opportunity to do this, I always took the picture and followed up with a proud fist pump, and they would enthusiastically yell, "Trump, Trump, Trump!" The sound of thousands in unison is deafening. It was so empowering, and my name isn't even Trump!

I can't imagine how inspiring it must have been for Trump to know he had the support of so many pushing him forward. Of course, while there were thousands behind him voicing their support, there were (and are) loud critics coming from another direction. We've heard the criticism: Trump is a narcissistic egomaniac. Trump is a racist bully. Or my personal favorite: Trump is stupid.

Trump is not a stupid man. If you felt he was doing something stupid, you usually needed to look a little deeper because he was probably up to something. It's been said: Donald Trump always looks like he's going to lose until just before he wins.

Anyone who has attained the level of success in life that Trump has is not under the assumption that it can be done without its critics. Nor do I believe he is thin-skinned enough to put too much worry in those attacks. In fact, if the man were motivated exclusively by those around him feeding his ego, he would have been quite content continuing the life he was leading.

Remember, Trump was *already* a celebrity adored and respected by many. If anything, his reputation—in the media at least—was better before.

But I don't believe he did this for himself.

Trump, like Jonah, was asked to act. Trump was driven to run. Because it was the right thing to do.

April 11, 2015—The campaign was not an official presidential campaign yet. (He didn't announce his formal run for the presidency until June of that year). Trump spent the day in Myrtle Beach, South Carolina. As you can imagine, everywhere he went people were asking him if he was going to run for president. Early on, like many presidential hopefuls, Trump spent a lot of time in South Carolina. It is a critical battleground state for Republican candidates, so it tends to get a lot of political visits. Many candidates focus their energy on the Palmetto State because doing well in the Republican primary is considered an early indicator of a candidate's strength.

Prior to this point, the crowds Trump had spoken to were part of bigger events. They had been larger conventions with a lineup of speakers, but on this day, he was the sole headliner. There were two events: The first one was extremely small, held at the Myrtle Beach Chamber of Commerce. There were no more than fifty people in the room. The second event was across town in a middle school gymnasium. There were an estimated five hundred in attendance at this event. Because it was at a middle school, members of the school band played as Trump entered the room. Listening to the school's marching band energized the audience, I remember him turning to his events coordinator and smirking, "Wow … I got my money's worth with you!"

During these earlier rallies, Trump was known to enter down the center aisle from the rear of the room. After a loudspeaker introduction, he walked through the crowd to take the front podium. He would high-five, shake hands, and accept the occasional selfie request. Trump's charisma was undeniable as I watched him shoulder to shoulder with a sea of thunderous, proud patriots.

Trump was used to speaking in front of big crowds, even in the political sense. He had given larger-scale speeches at CPAC (Conservative Political Action Conference) and the South Carolina Tea Party Convention to maybe a thousand attendees three months earlier. But on this day—on this first flight of solo campaigning—Trump was ingenious. He was intense, eloquent, and inspired. The fire roared.

The staff left that day reinvigorated. We knew that Trump was scheduled to be in Charleston, South Carolina, in two days, on Monday. After the intense showing we had just experienced, the adrenaline was turned up on the inside. We hung on his words, knowing at any point he would confess to the masses what America had long suspected, and he would acknowledge his run for commander in chief.

At six o'clock on Monday morning, I set out for Charleston, South Carolina, to attend Trump's next speaking arrangement. I live in Myrtle Beach, so it's a two-hour trip to Charleston by car. This left me plenty of time to question why I was charging in and offering my time when, perhaps, they may just send me home. At this early stage in the precampaign, there wasn't always the means to contact the proper channels for coordination. This wasn't an official run at this point, and there wasn't yet a chain of command. It wasn't unusual for me to get my assignment informally from an insider with event specifics. Almost always, it was extremely last minute. Knowing this, I would learn of an event and plan to attend before I was asked. On this day, specifically, I was not asked to cover the Charleston event. While I was not the photographer, I certainly *wanted* to be the photographer. I was desperate to prove my worth, show my unfailing support, and watch the history unfold before me. I was a team player, with or without pay. That is, of course, if they'd have me. It was a vulnerable position. I can only imagine there were moments that Trump felt the same way albeit on the grander scale: "I am willing to apply myself and give my best, but will you have me?"

If I felt out of place that day, I imagine Trump had to have felt the same.

Monday morning at nine o'clock was a sad departure from the Myrtle Beach event just two days earlier. I arrived early at the Charleston Chamber of Commerce, expecting a big crowd. There was not. I was one of the first arrivals. I did a double take to be sure this was the correct location; perhaps I had the wrong address. I had not. Once inside the chamber, I found the room we had been assigned. There was an unattended sign-in sheet on entry. By the time everyone had arrived, there were only about forty people in the room. There was no energy in the air—stone silent, pin-drop status. It was as if it were the first day of a college class, and everyone in the room was waiting for the professor to come in and slam down the syllabus. It was a far cry from the events of the previous day.

When Trump arrived, he could immediately sense the somber mood. He was led to a holding room before taking the stage. The room he'd been given had a door with a glass window that looked in on the sad crowd he was about to address. There was no way to avoid the lack of enthusiasm in the room. It was utterly deflating. In all my travels, for all the rallies and speeches I witnessed, this was the one and only time I saw Trump's energy drained by the surrounding circumstances. There was no applause, no music, and no excitement. Perhaps this was an instance when he was left introspectively wondering, "What in the world am I doing here? What in the world are *they* doing here?"

Halfway through the talk, Corey Lewandowski pointed at me with a stern index finger to approach him. As I crossed the room to him, I played his possible message in my head: "You weren't asked to be here. Don't photograph this. It's embarrassing. Go home. You're fired."

Unexpectedly, he told me to go to the next event.

Just twenty minutes away, at the Charleston Doubletree Hotel, Trump and soon-to-be Republican candidate Carly Fiorina would be speaking to a convention of state treasurers. One can't be certain whom to credit for pulling up the mood and straightening the mind-set. Donald Trump is a fierce competitor. It may have been the perception that competition materialized. It may have been the crowd being in tune with a tempo we were accustomed to. Regardless the creditor, this event breathed some life back into us. The depressed uncertainty of just an hour before washed away so quickly, it was a distant memory we were happy to bury.

The campaign was an up-and-down game. There were moments of the greatest confidence tangled with unfathomable uncertainty. If I was feeling it this far from the top, Trump, as sure as he is human, was questioning himself too. And that's okay. Every well-laid strategy begins with questions. Thankfully, uncertainty doesn't last forever.

Perhaps like Jonah, Trump was the reluctant messenger. So many times we watched him toss debris into the waters. The media, like the people of Ninevah, were violent and unrelenting. This campaign survived waves that could have sunk much greater ships, but Trump didn't blink after he accepted the course. While there were moments he was near drowning, someone was determined to see him through.

Mr. Trump said if a better captain had arrived, he would have happily handed over the helm. So perhaps He did, and he did.

> You hurled me into the deep, into the very heart of the seas, and the currents swirled above me … But you brought my life up from the pit, O Lord my God.
> —Jonah 2:3–6

Trump and me aboard what the staff all called "Trump Force One."

There were those on the staff that had been on the plane and bragged about it.
There were others who never set foot on the plane.
Access to Trump's plane was a Badge of Honor.
As it should be, this plane is just incredible.

Shortly after photographing Trump the first time,
I emailed one of the main advisors for the Trump team.
I provided them the pictures
that I had taken and offered my help.

One of those original first photos was this one.

What was amazing to me was not how
Mr. Trump reacted to the pictures,
but that he had at all.

The Trump Organization, at that time,
had more than 20,000 employees.
Still, he personally made time in his day
to thank me.

It was wonderful to see.
I was reminded that the true
character of a man is found in his action.

It is not revealed when he's in front of a crowd,
but by what he does when no one is watching.

TRUMP
THE TRUMP ORGANIZATION

Senior Vice President – Assistant to the President
725 Fifth Avenue | New York, NY | 10022
p.
trump.com

**From:** Sam
**Sent:** Wednesday, January 21, 2015 12:57 PM
**To:**
**Subject:** FW: Sam - Three pictures for Donald...

> To:
> CC:
> Date: Wed, 21 Jan 2015 11:56:23 -0500
> Subject: Sam - Three pictures for Donald...
> From: gene
>
> Dear Mr.
>
> This is Gene Ho.
>
>
>

Gene - Thanks - They are great -

# Chapter 3

### Joseph—Loyalty's Keeper

As morning dawned, the men were sent on their way with their donkeys. They had not gone far from the city when Joseph said to his steward, "Go after those men at once, and when you catch up with them, say to them, 'Why have you repaid good with evil?'" When he caught up with them, he repeated these words to them. But they said to him, "Why does my Lord say such things? Far be it from your servants to do anything like that!"
—Genesis 44: 3–7

I have been a wedding photographer all my adult life. Things have changed dramatically in the industry since my start in 1991. Seeing the evolution of photography make such dramatic leaps, while learning those curves and staying profitable, has not always been easy. It has come with more than its fair share of bumps and bruises.

Being an entrepreneur has been a labor of love and learning. This business has been like a child I had at twenty. It has been with me—a part of who I am—for more than half of my life. We grew up together. At times I cared so deeply for it, I was incapable of seeing its flaws. It has kept me up at night, ruined relationships, and drove me to question everything I know. Still, it's mine: my baby, my pride, and my passion.

Most small business owners will tell you what a relentless, tyrannical boss they have. The irrefutable truth is there is no one harder to work for than yourself.

One of the biggest hurdles was that my business existed a decade before the birth of digital. There was no manual for learning the transition into the new technology. It was a crash course, sink or swim. Once we phased out of film and settled into the digital world, the bottom line certainly improved. Admittedly, however, for a man who has dreamed big, the benefits weren't always apparent. Constantly growing the business became the only thing I saw—at times, losing the peripheral to remember perhaps someday I might like to rest, or I might be physically unable to keep this pace.

So things changed. Taking a lesson from my own coined photography niche, I saw things wide angle. Goals were altered. (Fatherhood happened.) Priorities were corrected. I realized I hadn't been breathing for years. I became grateful when I recognized that I already had everything I truly needed. I'd said for years, "Love what you do, and the money will follow." My mantra was always there. Now, with clarity, my life's goals needed only part of those words to live by: just "love what you do."

My business is an anomaly in the industry. Under my trademarked name, there have been years my staff boasted over thirty photographers. In those years, my group had not been the same steadfast employees. In fact, my business has survived four full revolutions of anarchy. At the end of each decimation, I still stood, camera in hand, insisting my will for it. I'd start again.

There were years you could open the phone book and peruse the yellow pages, and there was virtually not one photographer listed who hadn't started under my wing, having learned on my dime. I don't pretend to think I'm unique in that sense. Surely, there is a business owner of every imaginable profession reading that line, nodding in agreement.

Years ago, I remember listening to Dave Ramsey's radio show, and he said, "Who do you get to work for you when you're building from the ground? Anyone that will."

I learned that fit well for me. I've employed university-trained photographers, and while some were good, it normally came with more headache than benefit. There was a necessary deprogramming of sorts to bring them back to real-world applications. While it may be wildly nostalgic to have obtained the ability to develop an original black-and-white in the darkroom, my business couldn't employ that skill.

I found it was easier to take someone with heart, someone with a passionate desire to learn the craft with just a pinch of promising talent. That was my staff. The problem with this system boils down to one simple, human struggle: loyalty.

Two years—that's how long it would take for most of my understudies to achieve enough expertise to hold court. At this point they would begin shooting as the lead photographer at a wedding or event. For two years I afforded their flaws, covered for their shortcomings, and survived their ignorance. Yet through it all, I was building their confidence … you can see where this is going. Like clockwork, shortly after being crowned with a title, you could hear the buzzing in your ears as staff would talk among themselves. "Why in the world," they wondered, "would we stay here with this boss? We are perfectly capable of doing the same things without him. Probably better. He's not that smart, you know. Surely if Gene can do it, *anyone* can."

So the story would go more times than I can count. Despite the statistics screaming 80 percent of small businesses crash and burn! Despite the fact I could offer steady work and a reliable paycheck. Despite the fact I had poured all my knowledge into helping create what they'd become. This was quickly buried and excused as a self-serving duty.

Every desirable human quality hinges on the existence of loyalty. Without it, even the greatest is made lesser. The apostle Paul wrote:

And now I will show you the most excellent way …
Love is patient, love is kind.
It always protects, always trusts, always hopes, always perseveres.
Love never fails.
And now these three remain: faith, hope, and love.
But the greatest of these is love.
—1 Corinthians 13:1, 4, 7–8, 13

Love is the greatest, so much greater than we are. Love is glue that keeps us together, but love is beyond our control. Loyalty in it, we choose.

My wife says I am too quick to trust. She believes trust is earned, not given. I tend to believe, "I'll trust you until I can't." Maybe she's right, but it seems to be a lesson I haven't finished learning. Maybe I never will.

I introduce to you, Joseph, a man with a lesson in trust and loyalty. A man whose faith should have been shattered, but his loyalty to One never faltered.

**Meet Joseph**

The biblical Joseph most think of first is the husband of Mary—the earthly foster father of Jesus. He is not the Joseph I'm referring to here. The Joseph in this case is the son of Jacob—"The Amazing Technicolor Dreamcoat" Joseph.

Joseph was the eleventh son of twelve born to Jacob. However, Joseph was the first son born to Jacob's beloved wife, Rachel. Jacob viewed his young son as his favorite, showering him with special gifts, most notably the beautifully woven coat he wore. Joseph's jealous brothers had become restless with the displays of favoritism.

At the age of seventeen, Joseph shared a dream he'd had. In the dream his family was bowing down to him, Joseph, as their leader. If they had been jealous before, they were beyond words at this prospect. His prediction that he would one day rule over them was more than they could bear.

In their fury, Joseph's brothers plotted to kill him. The oldest of the brothers stepped in as the voice of reason, pleading that they not kill their brother. Instead, to be rid of him, they agreed to sell Joseph to some traveling gypsies. Then, taking his beautiful coat, they smeared it with blood to convince their father he'd been killed by wild animals.

For all the hurdles, Joseph would always find a way to make the best of the situation. Joseph was special.

Do you see someone skilled in their work?
They will serve before kings; they will not serve before officials of low rank.
—Proverbs 22:29

Even in the worst of times, Joseph was known for having the blessing of the Lord. He was recognized for his good and worked his way to the top time and again. Joseph's story is relatable to many of us in that the highs balanced with the lows in life. Joseph's road was strewn with betrayals against him. Eventually the deception of others led him to prison.

The resolve of Joseph is unparalleled. He continued to do what was right. He trusted freely. Among those whom he should have been safe, his own blood brothers had betrayed him.

In time Joseph rose above his circumstances and ended up as vizier in Egypt. In ancient Egypt, a vizier was the highest official under the pharaoh. In modern-day terminology, a vizier would be similar to the position of prime minister.

There are constitutional monarchies where the king is stripped of his powers. England and Spain are examples of this. There are also absolute monarchies, as in Saudi Arabia, where the king's decision is the law of the land. In both cases there is usually a prime minister who is ultimately the one calling the shots.

In many ways, this is similar to the president of the United States as well. While the president holds the highest office in the land, he is restrained by the other branches of government. And ultimately, a president, the living symbol of a nation, is also restrained by the will of the people.

One would think that a vizier or a prime minster would have more power if he or she served under a constitutional monarchy. After all, that would mean the king would have little real power. Depending on the situation, though, it is the vizier or prime minster of an absolute monarchy who would have more power.

How did Joseph rise to this level? In a time when kings became kings because their fathers were kings, he rose to the level of vizier when Joseph was a total outsider. He had no ties to the family. In fact, he wasn't even Egyptian; Joseph was an Israelite.

Joseph obtained his position because he was deemed a financial genius. It was by interpretation of a dream that he found his way into power.

The pharaoh had a dream:

> When two full years had passed, Pharaoh had a dream: He was standing by the Nile, when out of the river there came up seven cows, sleek and fat, and they grazed among the reeds. After them, seven other cows, ugly and gaunt, came up out of the Nile and stood beside those on the riverbank. And the cows that were ugly and gaunt ate up the seven sleek, fat cows. Then Pharaoh woke up.
> He fell asleep again and had a second dream: Seven heads of grain, healthy and good, were growing on a single stalk. After them, seven other heads of grain sprouted—thin and scorched by the east wind. The thin heads of grain swallowed up the seven healthy, full heads. Then Pharaoh woke up; it had been a dream.
> —Genesis 41:1–7

Joseph humbly told the pharaoh that he could not interpret the dream, but God would work through him to share the message. Joseph proceeded to interpret this dream, and doing so resulted in great prosperity for the pharaoh. The dream had to do with a veiled message: There would be seven fat years with great food production and successes. That would be followed by seven years of famine and struggle.

With this understanding, the pharaoh determined that while things were great, they should take those seven good years to save every scrap of food possible. That is exactly what they did. He was so relieved for the wisdom and understanding, the pharaoh put his trusted Joseph in charge of everything, saying, "Only with respect to the throne will I be higher than you." —Genesis 41:40

During the seven years of good times, they collected so much grain that they stopped counting it. They built silos to store it. While everyone thought that times were going to continue like this forever, Joseph knew it wouldn't.

Then, just as predicted, the famine came.

Through the pharaoh's trust in Joseph, he not only made it through the times of famine, but he prospered. People came from surrounding areas to buy the grain that was stored.

This is how much power Joseph had earned:

> The seven years of abundance in Egypt came to an end, and the seven years of famine began, just as Joseph had said. There was famine in all the other lands, but in the whole land of Egypt there was food. When all Egypt began to feel the famine, the people cried to Pharaoh for food. Then Pharaoh told all the Egyptians, "Go to Joseph and do what he tells you."
> —Genesis 41:53–55

The power Joseph gained by this was almost incomprehensible. He would go from being a complete outsider to the most powerful person in the land. Consider this: The Hebrews weren't even allowed to share a table with the Egyptians, yet Joseph was second in command.

Joseph didn't become a man of power without pain. His own brothers betrayed him to the point of selling him into slavery. He was lucky that a few had talked the majority out of killing him. Then he was falsely accused and spent years in prison. Still he managed to hold on to his faith and trust in God's plan for him.

The story continues. During the hardship of famine, the same ten brothers who had turned against Joseph traveled to Egypt. They were seeking to purchase grain from the governor of the land. They didn't realize it was their own brother who was now in command. After all the years that had passed, they had assumed he was dead.

It's hard to imagine the kind of pain Joseph must have carried. One would expect him to have become quite cynical after repeated betrayals. Through his years, he had come up with a system of discernment. He implemented tests to gauge the loyalty of those around him.

When his brothers came seeking grain from the pharaoh, they were unaware it was their own brother they faced, but Joseph recognized them. Still dear to his heart, he allowed them redemption and created a series of situations to test their honesty.

He agreed to make the sale and provided them with grain. Requesting transparency, he insisted they must return with their youngest brother to prove their honesty. Joseph then sent them on their way with the grain. Once home the men realized both the grain *and* the money to pay for it was in their bags. They were terrified; surely the vizier would think them to be frauds and thieves.

The famine continued, and it was necessary to seek grain from the pharaoh a second time. The brothers knew they could not return without their youngest brother, Benjamin. All these years later, but still heartbroken from the loss of Joseph, their father refused. With no food and no choice, they pleaded, eventually gaining their father's reluctant approval to approach Egypt's vizier once more—this time with their youngest brother in tow.

Again Joseph provided the grain. This time he planted a silver cup in the youngest brother's bag, and he sent them on their way. After leaving the city, Joseph sent his underlings after them. He commanded his staff to stop the brothers and search them, as one of them had "stolen" a silver chalice. Each man lowered his bag. From oldest to youngest, they were searched until reaching the end of the line. There they found the cup in Benjamin's bag. And Joseph's men said to them:

> Why have you repaid good with evil? Isn't this the cup my master drinks from and also uses for divination? This is a wicked thing you have done.
> —Genesis 44:4–5

When caught with the stolen item, Judah pleaded on behalf of the youngest brother, Benjamin. Seeing his siblings willing to trade their own lives to spare their young brother, they had passed Joseph's test.

In his eyes, they had redeemed themselves. They were rewarded for their truth and loyalty. Not only had Joseph forgiven them their earlier transgressions, but he also forgave them wholeheartedly. He ensured them it wasn't their fault; it had been God's will that they betrayed him, leading him down the path to one day be their salvation.

Joseph's story is a testament to the power of faith, loyalty, and trust. Through the challenges presented in his life, Joseph maintained a remarkable ability to forgive and carry forward. He had the wisdom to know that his siblings were imperfect, and he had the strength to leave their flaws in the past. Joseph understood their actions were necessary. Through them, the stage was set for a powerful story line of leadership and loyalty.

**Enter Trump**

One of the most commonly asked questions I hear, now that the dust has settled from the campaign trail, is what is Trump *really* like? Contrary to what they sell us on the front page, in my experience, he was fair, mild-mannered, and courteous. The way the media portrayed him through the campaign was most often painfully far from what I saw with my eyes. It became somewhat of a game for me to try to imagine what moment the critics might use on that day. I couldn't be sure whether to laugh or cry, seeing the way it would fall together in the headlines time and again.

Luckily, Donald Trump has a thick skin. We can assume he knew full well that this wouldn't be a Sunday afternoon stroll through Central Park. He was a unique presidential candidate in many ways, but one obvious difference was that he'd been a celebrity *before* he ran for office. At sixty-eight years old and much of that lifetime spent in the spotlight, he was familiar with the media wolf pack.

Donald Trump had built a public persona before taking the presidential podium. Some aspects of that celebrity image rang true for him as a candidate as well. One of the clichés that stuck was his famous phrase, "You're fired!"

While working alongside Trump, I can easily think of a half-dozen times I thought I would be on the receiving end of those words. That might seem like a lot, but these were high-stress situations. The resulting management turnover didn't foster confidence in a long-term position either. For me, the campaign environment was like nothing I had ever experienced. Neither would this historic campaign ever be duplicated. Mr. Trump's 2015–16 campaign run did not follow the traditional format of most modern campaigns. He refused to take money from the deep pockets, and he could afford to campaign without outside assistance.

Money was never a big motivation for me, except as a way to keep score. The real excitement is playing the game.
—Donald Trump

Knowing his reputation kept me on my toes. It was always my genuine desire to impress. I knew the highest levels of service were not only expected but also required. I was under pressure to master lighting situations at a glance. I had to remain respectful yet forceful enough to keep things moving. I sought out the most unique angles for displaying the masses in attendance. Everything was done while the clock ticked. I was good at it though. I enjoyed the pressure and was proud to have the talents to serve our country in this way.

I juggled an intense schedule that required travel and organization. Lest I forget, I had a business at home to tend to as well. I believe the pressure for greatness came mostly from Trump's management style. He tested those around him. He expected results that were nothing less than the best.

I take great pride in knowing I was taking photographs on both the first and last day of his campaign. There were certainly challenges along the way. Anything good is worth working for. I spent countless hours on the road. I had time to let my mind wander. Many times I felt there was a good chance I wouldn't be there tomorrow.

When anyone begins a new job, there's almost always some trepidation. In time, after learning the ropes and the structure, confidence settles in and a steady security replaces it. In two years, I never felt that security come. I didn't feel "safe" until about a month before the campaign's end. At that point, my service was no longer needed. All the high-impact images were made and had been reused numerous times, but I had made it.

There is a story from the middle somewhere in that familiar time of insecurity and self-doubt. It was the one time I was 100 percent certain that I was fired. Then afterward, if only for a fleeting moment, I felt like a worthy keeper, a trusted member within the campaign's chaos.

Once Trump won the Republican National Convention nomination, he did some fundraising for the Republican Party. This came much later in the campaign, near its end. With only a few months left before the election, we were at one such RNC event. The attendees had donated some serious cash to have a minute with Trump and a photograph made. This wasn't like the campaign rallies where random supporters may or may not have gotten a chance to meet and greet. These photos were necessary, and I would be responsible to a high-rolling donor if he or she didn't get a photo.

This was incredibly nerve-racking. As Donald Trump's photographer, the last thing I needed was a powerful, wealthy supporter complaining he or she didn't get a photo (or complaining that said photo was bad)!

On this day, there had been two formal events and a private meeting. I didn't have time to prepare my routine setup. It had been a race all day, from point A to point B. I had to quickly transition into the photo line.

Normally I didn't bring traditional studio lights because of the required setup and breakdown time. Logistically, with all things considered, lights were a burden more than a benefit. We would move so quickly to and from events that it simply wasn't feasible. I've always felt available light supersedes artificial options. Worst-case situations meant on-camera flash options were there to override the circumstances. But that day I had brought the clunky lights and bulky tripods they sit on, knowing I couldn't leave *anything* to chance.

Ultimately the boss at each event was Trump. However, after the evolution into official candidacy, each event had a "boss of the day," an event coordinator, or in our terms, the "lead advance." This person worked directly under Trump as the designated point of contact, in charge of making things run smoothly at that day's event. To complicate things a step further, each event often brought with it a new lead advance. The campaign had grown to the size that more people were necessary to cover the bulk of events we were running.

Some of our lead advance personnel had incredible workflow. It was obvious they belonged at the helm. Many of them were phenomenal to work with, grabbing a reputation that meant everything would go well under their charge. The flip side existed as well. Not all lead advances were born leaders. In some respects, they made the job harder and served as simply another body to dance around.

On this day, the lead advance was new. It was day 650-something for me, and I welcomed a fresh-off-the-street boss of the day. I had prided myself in the ability to move through the photo line quickly. My workflow was known among nearly all the other leads. Most of them were glad to step back and let the system work.

This day had started rough. We were behind on time, which wasn't unusual. I was aware and planned to compensate, to make up the time. We also had a long photo lineup that day, another hiccup I knew how to handle.

The new lead that day was dictatorial. "We don't need five clicks each. Just one click."

"I understand," I responded, somewhat shocked. I was grateful my face didn't reflect what I was thinking.

I pressed forward with the system we had been using. Following a well-vetted routine, I focused in and took three clicks of the shutter in rapid succession. Then I refocused and took two more. This added up to about fifteen seconds. It had been my routine since the start. Nearly two years had proven to me that it worked. I needed the extra frames. In a sea of people at speeds like this, the extra images ensured—in the most basic sense—that both parties had their eyes open in at least *one* of these frames. Then later, if needed, I was able to merge frames to make sure that whoever had stood with Donald Trump had their eyes *open* in said memento.

Two more passed through my line, and once again I heard, "One click. Do you understand?"

It was all I could do to hold my tongue. At this point, Trump had watched me march through these lines dozens of times. This had never been an issue. Now a random coordinator was implementing a maximum shutter trip of *one*?

I knew I was the convenient person for the new guy to push around. He busted my chops to declare his contributions to the day running smoothly. I couldn't help but think that Trump was entertained watching the attempted pyramid climbing. It was a painful display of unnecessary restraint.

That was when it happened.

As I struggled to survive the photo-line tyrant, cramped by my boss's snotty toady, with my nerves slowly reaching their peak—*crash!* Remember how I had said I didn't usually use lights? Add another reason to my list: tripping hazards! The entire stand was laid out on the floor in front of me.

I don't anger easily, but I was livid. Not for the equipment but for the lost time. My nerves were shot, thanks to Mr. Never Clickypants. I assumed it was my assistant's fault, and I immediately turned to spit fire in that direction.

As I did, I came face-to-face with Rudy Giuliani, the former mayor of New York. It immediately came clear: Rudy Giuliani had unintentionally ninja-spiked my lights into the ground.

This was a private room, no bigger than an average living room. Everyone heard. The entire room stood still (cliché pin drop). I was certain at this point the new lead advance was going to take me out back.

As Rudy untangled himself from the mess of light-stand legs and extension cords, and while I worked to regain my composure, Trump smiled as if nothing had happened. He was completely unfazed and ready to keep charging through the lineup. In that moment, I imagined Donald Trump as the dad who would utter, "Listen, if it's too hot for you, get out of the kitchen." I knew, by all of the eye contact exchanges during that split moment, I was all right. In the worst of it, Mr. Trump had faith that I had this under control. I kicked the light stand out of the way, and we kept firing frames. I quite liked the kitchen, and I could handle the heat.

••••••••••••••••••••••••••••••••••••••••••••••••••••••••••••

Mr. Trump is widely known for the value he puts on loyalty. And like Joseph, Trump is always testing those around him to gauge their true allegiance. The tests were sometimes subtle and other times more blatant. I suspect those public shows were meant for a truer read on his subject's reaction.

My job was stressful. No one was going to casually forget they'd had their photo taken with the presidential nominee. There was no room to miss a shot. There was no do-over or "see you all tomorrow," same time/same place.

To further push me out of my comfort zone, Mr. Trump routinely did something few people ever ask of me. He would ask to see the back of my camera, at the LCD screen. I would spontaneously be spot-checked, by the boss himself, on how my photos looked. Asked by anyone else, the answer was always a resounding no. No one sees the back of my camera as I'm working. That is, unless you're Donald Trump. Call it fear or call it pride. Call it humility, or call it my dutiful "yes, sir." I wasn't going to tell him no.

After a time or two of sharing with him, I realized quickly that what came next was a pat on the back and a chummy "good job, my man." However, I also faced the occasional sharp rebuke on lighting or even camera angle. Sometimes the critique was brutal, made worse when the critique was delivered in front of other people.

One instance I recall was especially humiliating. As usual, I was backstage. I'd had my lighting calculated. The backdrop had been set. I'd done my test shots and was prepared for the impending line. While we waited, Trump was giving an interview to a television station in the next room. We waited for him to finish. It was rarely, if ever, known to the people who were about to have their photo taken that *the* Donald Trump was on the other side of the wall, in the next room. But I knew.

I worked to stand out respectfully, his mainstay. I would stand to face the door he was slated to enter from. As usual, Secret Service walked in first, and Trump followed. As everyone cheered a welcome, Trump eagerly proclaimed, "Why don't we take pictures in the next room?"

Who's going to say no? *I'm* going to say *no*? Nope.

With my head reeling, we all walked into the adjoining room. My heart was racing because I had no idea what kind of lighting nightmare faced me on the other side of that door. Pin lighting, backlighting, fluorescents—what kind of potential headache of a light show awaited me?

I worked hard and fast to guesstimate where I would need to be for this new room, with the added pressure of one hundred enthusiastic Americans ready to have me make their photos great again. To take it up just one more notch of blistering stress, after the first frame, Trump asked to spot-check me. He asked to view the LCD screen on the back of my camera; of course I showed him. He didn't remark. We rushed to continue through the rest of the photo line.

When the photo line was finished, Ryan Fournier walked in for an impromptu meeting. Fournier, at the time, was the national chairman of Students for Trump. While he was a young man, he was exactly the kind of hardworking youth with enough clout that he could walk into a Trump event and manage his way into the meet and greet room.

He introduced himself and shared with Mr. Trump his accomplishments for the campaign thus far. As they closed their conversation, he took out his cell phone and asked if he could take a picture. Fournier handed his cell phone to someone in the room, and they stood for a photo together. Trump then asked to see his picture—yes, the one on the cell phone.

Trump took a quick look at it and said, "See … this is good. Not like *this* guy," as he shook his thumb in my direction. I laughed. I was glad we were at a level of comfort that he knew he could throw a couple elbows in my ribs here and there. But in reality, I was humiliated.

I felt like crawling into a hole. I had been tested. I failed. Forget being fired. I really wanted to ride off into the sunset, with a six-pack of Bud, to attend a pity party—for one.

When everyone left the area, I approached Trump privately.

"Mr. Trump, I know I didn't have those first frames right, but please know I'll fix it," I said.
With a repeated nod, he said two simple words to me: "I know."

While I had been publicly checked and subsequently humbled, I couldn't help but realize he had a marked faith in me. Perhaps I had passed after all. I know my craft. I promised to make it right, and Trump trusted fully that I would.

And I think I have.

All the buzz on the campaign trail was that no matter how big the arena, Trump crowds would fill the stadium. But Trump crowds would also fill a farm.

The black and white photo below is the line entering the property.
The line went a half mile in one direction, turned and continued another half mile in the other direction.

At bottom: Once inside the cozy barn, Trump gave his talk in his signature Red Cap. Down on the farm, and flanked by hay bales, Secret Service also "dressed down."
They didn't wear a tie.

Above: This talk was one of the first rallies that cable television channels broadcasted live.
This photo was taken as he exited, from an angle to the side of the stage that was restricted to the public.
It shows the more solemn side of Trump.

Left: In more familiar fashion...
An early campaign photo shows Trump in a swamp of excited supporters.
His energy and passion were infectious.

# Chapter 4

## Ehud—The Artful Redeemer

After Ehud had presented the tribute,
he sent on their way those who had carried it.
But on reaching the stone images near Gilgal he himself went back
and said, "Your Majesty, I have a secret message for you."
The king said to his attendants, "Leave us!" And they all left.
—Judges 3:18–19

Years ago, I had a great conversation with a friend who had made his living as a career waiter. When I say career waiter, I mean he hadn't been working as a waiter to bide time as he put himself through college. He was working, successfully, at a high-end restaurant in a tourist-driven city, powered by a service-industry economy. He had consistently made good money primarily credited to his ability to earn tips.

In chatting, I noted his success and commented how difficult it must be to always be "on." I questioned him about what a challenge he must face having to be cheery all the time. After all, I thought, being sunny and upbeat is the key to pulling in great tips. Right?

He gave me a one-sided grin and smoothly said, "Nope, wrong." He had found that the key to making great tips had little to do with bubbly optimism. He then gave me an education that I will never forget. "Quite the opposite," he proceeded. "The key to making great tips is to be just a *little* irritated."

He continued to explain how it worked night after night. On the first visit to a new table, he would intro with the typical, expected greetings—a hearty welcome, mundane weather comments, and "Is this your first time with us?" Everything was predictably scripted, the same as every other waiter they had ever had—comfortably forgettable, routine, and familiar.

Then, on one of the early check-ins with his new friends, he would casually and lightly mention how frustrated he was on this day. It was someone else to blame, you know …

"Can I grab you another water? I tell you—I'm bumping them along back there in the kitchen. Please be patient with me. They aren't backed up, but they are moving soooo slow tonight. I apologize in advance. I'll stay on them. I'm going to bring you out some bread here in just a second. Y'all have any questions?"

In other words, "Dear friends, *we* are on the same team. It's you and me versus the kitchen. Not the kitchen and me versus you."

Before the night's end, each table was endeared to him. After all, he made sure their table had a lovely evening, despite the chaos in the kitchen. Their meal was not only timely but also cooked to perfection! Their dedicated waiter endured the kitchen's lagging, was pleasant throughout, *and* he kept them informed with insider info. He deserved a great tip. What a super guy!

Ta-da! A con? Theatrics? Lies? Manipulation? Label it any way you want, as long as you don't omit: effective.

I think most people employ a similar degree of cunning in life, perhaps not always with the financial gain. Think about the last time you were in a car while someone was being pulled over for a minor infraction.

Let the games begin! Raw human response. Undoubtedly, there are cops out there who could write a book on the colorful ways people attempt to steer themselves out of a speeding ticket. We humans are masterful creators of calculated untruths, especially with a set of cherries and berries in the rearview.

First, there is the outright lie: You make no attempt to con yourself in the process. You're comfortable in it.

I had a friend who, upon being pulled over, insisted to the officer that she had to use the restroom. She got specific, as lies often go, sharing far more information than necessary. Yes, she divulged, it was of the, ahem, secondary nature. Nothing like the inclusion of humiliation to inflate a shameless lie. She was embarrassed, and he was embarrassed; they couldn't even look one another in the eye after she said it. Yet, as you can guess, it didn't work. The seasoned officer kindly replied, "Okay, I'll follow you to the nearest rest stop … and I'll wait."

Then there's the little white (but still a) lie: You want to believe you're honest. For that you attempt to con yourself.

"Hello, Officer! No, I'm not sure why you pulled me over. Did I do something wrong? Headlight, maybe? Oh, goodness how fast was I going? Hmm, was it … I'd say fifty-six or fifty-seven, maybe?" You reply as though it was lost on you that you might be speeding as you tore past three cars like they were standing still. Also lost will be the pad of friendly "warning tickets" when Sergeant Smells BS gets back to his patrol car. A lie is a lie, even sold as ignorance.

On occasion a news report will come out with a celebrity using the haughty classic, "Do you know who I am?" I can't imagine that kind of brazen arrogance ever being successful. For as often as it's used, it must work sometimes. What an unfortunate turn when the officer lowers his aviators, narrows his eyes, and slowly swings his head, saying, "No, nor do I care. License and registration."

Full confession, I have my own method. No shame in my game—we all have our tried and true. My routine is the supercompliant guy. Truth be told? Works quite well. My wife hates that I don't get ticketed. She thinks it's because I'm somehow working connections. That's not my secret. I'm just a good, old-fashioned butt kisser. When I get pulled over, I put down all windows, keep both hands on the wheel in plain sight, and respectfully ask permission before I reach down to retrieve my driver's license. I am overly polite, ultra-patient, and entirely apologetic.

Am I being manipulative? I suppose it depends who you ask. I don't like getting ticketed. I like even less hearing "I told you so" from my wife. Note to self: perhaps I have a little too much personal experience perfecting the "art of a traffic stop."

Traditionally, cunning and manipulation tend to be thought of as negative qualities. It's generally assumed that one cannot be godly *and* be skilled in trickery. However, while everyone remembers Jesus's famous comment in Matthew 10:16, "I am sending you out as sheep among wolves," we cannot overlook what he said next: "Therefore be as shrewd as snakes."

I realize Jesus wasn't instructing us to lie to get out of a traffic ticket or swindle a table to secure a bigger tip. But being artfully cunning? That is a principle that is mentioned biblically for both good and bad.

If you were to consider how being cunning played a negative role in the Bible, ask yourself who the most deceitful biblical character may have been. I'm sure Judas would probably come out on top. He's certainly a worthy contender for the title. However, he wasn't terribly stealthy.

Jesus knowingly said to His disciples, "One of you will betray me." One by one they replied mournfully, "Surely not I, Lord?"

Judas had already accepted a bribe to betray Jesus yet joined in saying, "Surely not I, Lord." Judas fooled some, but he hadn't fooled Jesus.

Let me share with you a story from the scriptures about a man used by God—one who may very well be in the running for most cunning. This is trickery and wit used to achieve the will of God. This is a man whose deliberate act of deceit ushered in the liberation of God's people.

This is the story of Ehud.

**Meet Ehud**

Ehud was the second in a line of twelve judges of Israel. These times, after the death of Joshua, were Israel's dark ages. The Israelites, in their moral depravity, strayed from God time and again. Each time God sent them judges to lead them in righteous living.

A judge in that time was a military hero, a freedom fighter, sent to rescue and guide God's people. The judges were men (and one woman) who were strong leaders, raised up by God to inspire the Israelites and set their hearts back to Him.

During the time of the judges in Israel, there was no king. In fact, there was no real government at all. The tribes of Israel in Ehud's time were under occupation by Eglon, the king of Moab. Because Israel was under Eglon's control, Israel had to make a tribute (pay taxes) to this foreign king. Make no mistake; the Israelites didn't willingly give their tax to Eglon. The Israelites were enslaved. This hadn't been for merely a year or two; they had been under the enemy tyrant for eighteen years. Work and pay taxes, and in exchange, the Israelites were allowed to live. Desperate for relief and anxious to repent, the people of Israel cried out to the Lord for help. God gave them Ehud.

Ehud had one burning motive as a judge: to liberate his people from the eighteen-year oppression. To do so he devised a rather cunning plan. As judge, it was Ehud's duty to deliver the tribute to the foreign king. Ehud likely began by carefully laying the groundwork of trust between him and Eglon. Certainly, having his presence associated with a host of riches helped his cause.

Ehud and his entourage proceeded to the king's attendance with the tribute offerings. Ehud, as judge, was a man of power. Therefore, it was customary that he would be accompanied by his own group of bodyguards. After they laid out the tribute before the king, he sent his men on their way. Ehud also left the palace.

We can only speculate why Ehud and his men left at that point. Perhaps Ehud had allowed his men blissful ignorance. He gave them the opportunity to be well enough away from the palace that they might be safe from what he had planned. Maybe Ehud had left, having second thoughts about the savage act he had been plotting. Whatever the reason, Ehud left the palace only to return a short time later. This time he was alone.

Prior to the delivery of the tribute, Ehud had crafted a small, double-edged dagger. The construct was just one foot long, small enough to conceal it strapped to his thigh and small enough not to restrict his normal gait. Before Ehud approached the king a second time, he took his dagger along.

Surely the king's security ensured a thorough pat-down the first time Ehud had been in to see the king. Since the majority of the population was right-handed, men were versed in seeing a sword on the left hip. However, Ehud was left-handed, and his dagger was concealed on his right thigh. This could possibly explain the oversight. It may be that it was simply overlooked since he had been in to see the king just moments earlier. Maybe the second frisking was less aggressive. It could be that they didn't check at all. After all, he hadn't been an issue just moments ago. Additionally, he had returned without his protective guards. This, too, could have lowered the fear of attack.

Gaining entry with the dagger in tow was only half the battle. The king's men remained at his guard.

For what happened next, you need to use a little imagination to bring it to life. His body language must have been brilliant in selling the act—hands clasped in innocence, head down, and chin to the side. I can imagine him cleverly signaling the king with his eyes how paramount this special message was when he said intriguingly, "I have a secret message for you, O king."

Perhaps the old king had lowered his guard after nearly two decades of this routine. It was said the king was a very heavy man. It may be that he viewed Ehud as smaller and therefore weak. Or maybe it was nothing more than a moment of poor judgment. Whatever the reason, the king commanded his bodyguards, "Leave us!" The men left the room, and Ehud and Eglon stood alone in the king's quarters.

I imagine they nodded to one another approvingly as the king's brute squad left the room, both understanding the plight of handlers. Ehud then stretched out with his right hand to offer a firm shake. At the same time, he went for the dagger with his dominant hand and stabbed Eglon, killing him.

After Ehud murdered the king, he escaped unseen. You should read for yourself how he bought the time to get away (Judges 3:24).

The story of Ehud details how cunning he was in carrying out his conspiracy. The chapter concludes by sharing the favorable product of his bold actions and inspired leadership: "and the land had peace for 80 years."

**Enter Trump**

Politician \pä-lə-ti-shən\ (noun): a person *involved in influencing* public policy and decision-making.

Politics is about being cunning. Period.

Government has a rotten reputation: scheming and self-serving, scandals and broken promises, shameless exploitation, and routine abuses of power. Most of us have not lived a day of our lives without a presidency that can be called corrupt and riddled with conspiracy and unscrupulous drama. From the magic bullet of 1963 to cigars in the oval office … so much secrecy and shame.

America has gotten so accustomed to the neglect that we've gone to sleep. Exhausted and defeated, our eyes open each day and go to work, polluted and robotic. We let the powers that be control our fate, believing change is too far out of our reach and out of our control.

By his own admission years ago, Donald Trump wanted no part of this mess. Thankfully he took to the podium and shared his contagious patriotism. He believed in America and knew it could be what it was meant to be: of the people, by the people, and for the people.

Once Donald Trump resigned himself to taking on the challenges of running for United States president, he played with the best of them. In fact, Trump vanquished the lineup of the world's most crafty career politicians. One of the chief masters of the craft is Ted Cruz. He is a lawyer and seasoned in the political realm.

There are many battlefields in a new-age campaign. Who can survive the mainstream media? Who can dominate social media? One of the biggest battles is being capable of conveying thoughts and policies in a live debate. One of the most unsung campaign battlefields are conventions, where there are multiple speakers in succession. These conventions aren't always televised, but they are wildly valuable because candidates have a chance to win over a specific segment of the voting populace. Examples of these conventions include the big ones like CPAC (Conservative Political Action Conference) and small ones like the National Conference for State Financial Officers. At the latter, candidates like Trump and Carly Fiorina spoke in the spring of 2015. This convention fit in a hotel ballroom and was attended by the nation's state treasurers and their staffs. The motivation was an opportunity to win over the endorsement of each treasurer and to position themselves as the financial candidate.

Most of the more brutal battles at these conventions go on behind the scenes, between staffers. Logistics, such as time slots and which day a candidate will speak, make a decided difference. So, when accepting an invitation to one of these events, specifics like who speaks before/after whom and on which day are deeply negotiated. No potential presidential candidate wants to speak just before lunch to a hungry, unfocused crowd. Neither does a candidate want to be viewed as the "opening act" of another.

Unlike the televised debates, there are no public discussions or media dialogue on a winner or loser; still the candidates are incredibly competitive. Each time out is an opportunity to earn votes by emerging as the perceived winner.

One such event is the smaller but still influential South Carolina Tea Party Coalition Convention. In 2015, Trump and Cruz attended this convention. At the time neither were officially a candidate for president. It was a classic case of political cat and mouse.

Cruz spoke first, polished to the line. He looked and spoke like a statesman. He was friendly but formal. He was dominant and controlled, and he overall gave a powerful, official-feeling performance.

The next day was Trump's turn to speak to the same crowd. Trump took a different strategy entirely. He took to the stage in a fanatical flurry of high fives. He was inviting and approachable, doling out double thumbs-up and fist pumps. He spoke like an old friend on a porch swing. He took to the middle of the crowd and came off as approachable, charming, and down to earth. He was everyman that day. He left those lucky enough to garner a fist bump a story they're likely still sharing today.

This is, of course, subjective, but I believe Trump won this convention. It was genius. It would be very difficult to out-politician the politician in seasoned US senator Ted Cruz. So Trump didn't bother to try. Why fight fire with fire when water works much better?

That was 2015. In 2016, the battle would be had all over again. The two would duke it out at the same convention, just a year later. Only this time the stakes were much higher. By now the election cycle was in full swing, and both Trump and Cruz were upper-echelon Republican candidates.

Again it was Cruz who spoke first, this time taking to the room as the proverbial guy next door. He went straight "Tim the Tool Man" with coffee and a newspaper. It was a brilliant political move. Cruz stole a page from the playbook that led to Trump being favored the previous year.

How in the world was Trump going to counter? In January 2016, Trump had already been put under Secret Service protection. Cruz had not yet. Ted Cruz could walk anywhere he pleased and rub elbows with the masses, without restriction. Cruz saw this as an opportunity and took it. Trump, on the other hand, being under protection of the Secret Service, was unable to crowd-surf his way into the people's hearts. There was virtually no way to be more personable than Ted had been when girded by men in black.

Never underestimate the instinctive, cunning actions of Donald Trump. What he did next was pure genius.

Trump, being Trump, thought big. He went into full presidential mode. He gave an extraordinarily patriotic talk. He stressed the importance of a clever negotiator, willing to fight and insistent on winning. He delivered his mission statement with confidence and promise. His speech was organized and thorough, yet he conveyed the message without talking over heads or coming across as condescending. He looked the part, spoke the part, and left no question: he was prepared for the position of commander in chief. He was a man on a mission, set to deliver a message on the direction of the country. A man there to provide his hopes for what was to be done. Once complete, he waved a stately hand and was whisked out through a bevy of camera flashes. This was our president.

Outside of the convention that day, a group of Harley riders called "Bikers for Trump" lined the streets to greet Trump's motorcade. These bikers with their leather and noise lined the entrance/exit of the hotel. With their pro-Trump signs, they paraded their support proudly. It was a sight to see. The line stretched almost half a mile. As the motorcade passed by, they thundered with approval. Many of them were veterans and stood at salute. If this had happened a year earlier, there was no doubt in my mind that Trump would have stopped and given them a hearty thank-you. From inside the limo, he saw them. Impressed by such a gathering, surely a proud smile spread across his face as he humbly nodded approval. Of the people, by the people, and for the people.

As to whether or not Trump won that day, it would seem the dots connected. The confirmation came a month later when he won the South Carolina Republican primary.

• • • • • • • • • • • • • • • • • • • • • • • • • • • • • • • • • • • • • • • • • • • • • • • • • • • • • • • • • • • •

Trump was (and is) an ingenious strategist in planning and execution. Besides being cunning, Donald Trump was a master of inspiration. He drove people to believe. He was able to motivate those around him to work endless hours by leading the charge. We did so excitedly, as those of us on the inside believed with unwavering conviction that he was the right man for the job. He had the confidence to believe he could pull off the impossible. Parts of him, at times, may have even felt like Ehud, that he could do it alone. It seemed he was always two steps ahead of the opposition, knowing his counterstrategy before he'd applied the initial move.

Remember, there's no such thing as an unrealistic goal
—just unrealistic time frames.
—Donald Trump

From firsthand experience, I can tell you that Trump knows how to get things accomplished. He operates with intuition, and he's clever enough to get what he needs out of people.

As with any job, when you slip up, you hope the boss doesn't notice. I'm the first to admit—as hard as I tried—not everything I did for Trump was flawless. Recalling one of these blunders takes me to a time when I was running through our meet and greet photos. I snapped the photo, gave a "Thank you very much" to the gentleman, and, per routine, directed him to the door.

Trump stopped me bluntly. "You didn't get the picture. You missed it."

A little taken aback, I paused. Certainly I listened. I composed myself. I steadied my camera and took three more shots to make sure I'd gotten the frame.

There's a chance that Trump was posturing for this man. Maybe he made a show of how important the moment was to capture. By demanding a redo, he suggested it mattered just as much to him too. There is also the chance that Trump was hyperaware of the rhythm of the routine we had, and that he had a gut feeling.

Either possible explanation is brilliant, but what's more, when I reviewed my pictures later, I realized he was right. When I lowered my camera the second time, Trump grinned. "There! Now you got it!"

I think most people simply want to be treated fairly. When we do well, we'd like to be acknowledged for that. When we don't, we can take the criticism. Trump was easy to dish out the praise and quick with corrective criticism.

Late in the campaign, I was given an opportunity to showcase what I do best. The story is the same one: meet and greet photos behind on time. While shooting the last VIP, about twenty additional people walked into the room. The look on Trump's face told me that he hadn't been made aware of the group, and he was scanning the room for the responsible party.

If there was ever a time in the campaign that I anticipated what was going on, this was the time. Groups, particularly ones that large, didn't just show up unannounced. I quickly deduced it had to have been family. I was right. Since they were extended family members by marriage, Mr. Trump hadn't recognized the first folks through the door. Bringing in the tail of the group was his son, Eric Trump, with wife Lara.

During a few quick introductions and hugs, I had already switched lenses and prepared to run my game. If there is one skill I have confidently mastered as a wedding photographer, it's the ability to manage chaos and get a group shot done—and fast.

This is probably the only time during the campaign that I took 100 percent control of the floor. It was mine. It didn't matter that I was too close or moving too erratically. It didn't matter that the lead advance was probably going to yell at me. This was the only time during the campaign that I insisted on doing things my way.

Moving like a seasoned pro, I lined up the group and made sure everyone looked good. I barked orders like Tom Brady giving an audible at the line of scrimmage. "Okay, I can't see you … forward a little. On the end, move to your left a touch. Everyone, eyes here. Smiles!"

If there was ever a time that Trump was proud of me, it was in that moment. It was a simple gesture, but that's all it takes sometimes. Simple acknowledgments. When through, he gave me a big slap on the back and boasted, "That's my guy! Very nice!"

Things for me weren't always great, but Trump knew where the end of the rope was. He knew when to pour a little more in, so I had the will to continue. Whether he cared about me personally or just needed me to do the job, whatever the reason, Trump always managed to give just enough to keep me around.

A con? Theatrics? Lies? Manipulation? Label it any way you want as long as you don't omit: effective.

Trump knew how to charm people. He was very much like Ehud in his clever presentation, cunning nature, and persuasive ways. He knew how to motivate those around him to get the job done. Virtually everyone around him felt like I did. We worked hard for him, knowing ultimately it was for America.

Whatever the driving force was that brought it out of us, he deserves credit for holding it all together. He was brilliantly convincing in raising the belief that we could truly make America great again. We should all be so lucky for this chapter of history to conclude like Ehud's: sharing the favorable product of his bold actions and inspired leadership.

"Diamond & Silk" - two extraordinary women and
a wonderful example of the power in an unrelenting voice.

They are the example of women I hope my own daughters
will grow up to be one day.

Diamond & Silk led the charge; with their back-and-forth
commentary and independent thinking.
I was lucky enough to share time with D&S
and it is my great honor to call them friends.

Rarely did the media show what was really going on at the rallies.

It was like going to a sporting event!
Vendors would line the streets. They would sell Trump hats, shirts and pins.
Patriotism came too, free of charge.

On rally days, if the scheduled start time was 4pm, people would begin lining the streets at about 7am.

Those who lined up earlier would get the better seats and the greatest chance of getting an autograph or a selfie in the post-rally "rope line".

# Chapter 5

## Abner—Commander of Influence

At these words of Ishbaal, Abner flew into a rage.
"Am I a dog's head?" he shouted ...
Ishbaal dared not to say a single word to Abner in reply to him,
because he was afraid of him.
—2 Samuel 3:8, 3:11

Somewhere along the line in modern-day culture, we decided that vocalizing our beliefs is disrespectful to others. You may, of course ... if you're prepared for the label that comes with it.

This phenomenon didn't happen overnight. It was a slow spiral—a gasp, then a whisper, a wide-eyed stare, some long-winded blogs, *way* too much time for dwelling, and a few lawsuits. So was birthed the idea that we must all carefully fall into a position of being perfectly and properly politically correct. In large part, this drove Trump's campaign success. Without too much tiptoeing or hesitation, Trump has said *exactly* what is on his mind, even if saying it wasn't the popular thing. This is in stark contrast to the droves of politicians we've been accustomed to, smiling in our faces and telling any crooked lie necessary to gain voters and approval.

Interestingly, political correctness has been around so long, it has spawned a younger, hipper problem child. Political correctness is now also known via "microaggressions." For those lucky enough not to have heard of this concept, microaggressions are said to be the verbal and nonverbal insults that communicate hostility.

The University of California recently created a guide on these offenses. In the guide, it notes that phrases like "America is the land of opportunity" and "I believe the most qualified person should get the job" are discriminatory statements.

We're left in a place with no winners. We've gone from the position that everyone gets a trophy to the belief that no one deserves to win. Either way, the prevailing message for youth is "strive for mediocrity."

For quick reference, Oxford Dictionary's definition of *political correctness* is this:

The avoidance of forms of expression or action that are perceived to exclude, marginalize, or insult groups of people who are socially disadvantaged or discriminated against.

The biggest struggle with reconciling this is understanding that when *perception* is involved, things get a little fuzzy around the edges. You see a shade of blue that looks gray to others. I believe if we're all being honest with ourselves, we can probably agree it comes down to this, as a whole:

We don't empathize.

Everyone is discriminated against by everyone for everything. We are deplorable for standing with the candidate we support. We're chastised for what we believe and how we believe it. We are noted for any color package we were born into and how much money we have (or don't have). We're shamed for what we eat or choose not to eat. We are watched if we have an accent. We envy our neighbors and cut one another on social media. The amount of hate is unending, but it's *so much easier* to just be nice.

We need to start talking. We need to educate ourselves. We need to be intellectually honest and choose our words more softly. We need to learn to shrug when we don't agree, admit when we're wrong, and *apologize more freely*.

Discrimination, in its simplest form, is to hate difference. Ironically, difference is what makes this place so beautiful. Palm trees, live oaks, Japanese maple, birch and sequoia—how brilliant that we can go out into the world every day and appreciate difference on a basic level. Imagine how much more so if we learned to *acknowledge* an appreciation for difference—in all forms.

Quite simply put, if you don't like bonsai trees, you don't have to. Bonsai trees don't have to affect your life or the attitude you carry into it. You can go home smiling to a bonsai-free zone.

To complicate things further, society has additionally determined that we shouldn't demonstrate anger. Let me be clear; there is a difference between anger and violence. We're made to think we should be ashamed of an inability to keep calm. So we medicate to numb and we stand idle.

I'm not to say it's right or wrong, but there's something to be gained in facing and feeling anger and *unloading* what you feel. It's deeply honest, cathartic, and progressive to speak your mind freely. If you accomplish nothing else, you've opened the door to conversations—conversations with opposing views and similar views and everything in between. All to consider respectfully and without shame, understanding there is a time to agree you disagree. It's for those willing to put everything on the table so things can change, and successes are made.

There is no doubt that Trump was (and is) one of these people. It was often the one thing supporters appreciated and found most refreshing with him as a candidate. Not everyone agreed, but many respected him simply for bravely saying what he thought and having the conviction to stand behind those words. Certainly, there were moments he may have wished he chose his words differently. Such is to be human.

One of the resounding expressions I heard from patriots on the trail was that while they loved the majority, they didn't agree with him on *all* issues. The odds are slim that people are going to have a candidate who fits every single chosen platform to a tee. These sentiments were probably noted, in part, to distance them from some of the more controversial comments Trump made. Regardless, most everyone I spoke to about Trump said they appreciated that he spoke without fear or restraint.

I think the big problem this country has is being politically correct.
I've been challenged by so many people,
and I don't frankly have time for total political correctness.
And to be honest with you, this country doesn't have time either.
—Donald Trump

Reflecting on this campaign, I think about the times I lost my patience. Frankly, sometimes I wish I had lost it more often. Perhaps losing my cool *every once in a while* would have garnered me more respect.

In the very beginning, it was only Trump and his main bodyguard, Keith Schiller. Presidential candidates don't typically have bodyguards when they begin campaigning. In fact, in my memory, the only other active candidate I saw with protective detail at that time was Governor Rick Perry of Texas. Most likely this was due to him being a sitting governor.

As the campaign grew, Trump's personal team did as well, adding more bodyguards and crew members. Schiller handpicked most of these new bodyguards. Many of them were ex-NYPD. One undeniable observation was they were all massively colossal men.

I remember working the first event after Trump officially announced his run. The whole nation was talking about his comments regarding Mexico. No doubt, the threats were at a high. Mr. Trump came on site with a team of bodyguards that looked like (an even more intimidating version of) the front line for the Green Bay Packers. I will never forget Schiller walking in at Trump's side, both flanked by these towering bodyguards. Keith Schiller went down the line, at a distance, quietly updating the new recruits by pointing out individuals in the room, "He's good. She's good." Then he jerked a thumb to me. "He's good too." Phew,

(On a personal note: I have so much respect for Mr. Schiller, and to have his nod of approval was/is an immense compliment.)

After working a few events, I was also able to form relationships with the newer bodyguards. They would be dispatched to their positions before Trump's arrival. While we waited, I would pass the time by talking with them. This was one of the best periods of time for me during the campaign. While the campaign was blossoming, I had all the access I needed to get the photos I wanted, with little to no restrictions.

However, shortly after Trump's announcement to run for the presidency, his homegrown security team was quickly replaced with official Secret Service detail. For the most part, staff was thrilled that Secret Service was involved. This, after all, was what we aspired to from the beginning: for things to gain traction and get real. And it did—fast. It was an interesting transition, not without its stresses and growing pains.

The introduction of Secret Service changed the dynamics of our little "family" quite substantially. Prior to Secret Service, Mr. Trump's personal bodyguards primarily maintained his security. These were bodyguards at the highest levels, and it was always the same group. After the takeover of Secret Service, many of Trump's personal bodyguards got shifted to event security. This made them virtual outsiders comparatively.

Secret Service was responsible for one objective only: the safety of the person they guarded. I can imagine the United States government found it easier to step in and take over than to merge its forces with Trump's existing staff. Perhaps that would compromise their objective in some way. There wasn't a manual to follow. Prior to this point, there had never been a candidate who employed such an extensive security team without the help of the US government.

The Secret Service did an incredible job. How fluidly they moved and communicated to keep the presidential hopeful's safety was extraordinary to watch in action.

With Secret Service taking over, the game changed. It felt like a demotion to all of the staff. There was so much to relearn in the middle of the game. One of the most obviously felt changes involved security clearance.

Unfortunately, at events of this scale, having clearance wasn't always as easy as scanning a uniform badge or a passcode. Secret Service divided up an area into subsections. Merely walking from front corner to front corner of the stage, I may have been crossing over to another Secret Service officer's territory and therefore needed to confirm my access again. It's understandable that there were required layers of access. Admittedly, though, it created quite a binding system for those of us working, particularly those who needed to move. It was a huge struggle for me, as I needed to roam the room to find the best angles to photograph during the live event.

My struggles were mainly with some of the midlevel Trump staff who were new to the scene. Some were incredible to work for; they immersed themselves into the mix and hit the ground running. Others weren't so easy. With the power to grant or withhold access, a few took great pleasure in exercising the power to deny—if for nothing else than to exercise their right.

There were three levels of access: hard, soft, and restricted. Hard access was free reign to go anywhere, cross any line. A perfect example would be Mr. Trump's family members, campaign management, and his closest advisers.

Soft access meant we could freely walk past checkpoints. Soft access had great control; we could vouch for someone and escort the person through a checkpoint quickly.

Restricted was a level down from soft. With restricted access, we were free to travel within *most* territories but unable to escort another through. Restricted was the lowest access granted. The only lower access level was for those who were permitted backstage but had to be supervised. For example, a VIP for a photo or a local speaker needed to be escorted in and out of various locations since they lacked an access level.

Hard-access individuals were few and far between. But the roulette table came into play at soft access. Our level of access changed from location to location. Whoever was lead advance that day (and what kind of mood he or she were in) determined the day's clearance. They had now become Trump's gatekeepers.

Each event started with me checking in with the day's lead advance. Depending on who was in the position on that day made some events great and others more challenging. This brings me to the one time on the campaign trail that I almost completely lost my composure:

It went down as the one day on the campaign that I wish I would have been more forceful. It was shortly after the official announcement. The staff was getting used to the Secret Service. On this day, for whatever reason, the lead advance gave me no clearance. I wasn't given soft access. I wasn't given restricted access. I was granted no clearance. If he could have revoked my access to the parking lot, he might have done so.

That meant I needed to be babysat everywhere I went. I needed someone to walk me backstage. I needed someone at my side as I set up for the VIPs. I had a babysitter at the restroom. It was humiliating, if I can be honest. I'd been with Trump for months at this point, and now this fresh-off-the-street lead advance was challenging my ability to do the job. Mostly it was a way for him to wield the mighty newfound power. I realized that—even then. It was incredibly frustrating to grin and bear it, but I did, and I didn't complain.

When Trump arrived for VIP photos, we ran through them quickly before he took stage to speak.

This is where things went to Crazytown.

Once I had finished the meet and greets, I needed to make my way back to the rally area. The live pictures of Trump on stage, speaking to the crowd, were considerably more valuable to the campaign than the meet and greet portraits were. I couldn't find anyone with soft clearance to walk me back. I knew there were two routes back to the stage. The first route was back through the building, which was a twisted maze—and I hadn't left a trail of bread crumbs. Not to mention, I knew along the way that I would have to stop at each checkpoint and for that would likely miss the first half of his talk.

What I decided to do was take the quick and easy way back. I could skip *all* the checkpoints if I left the building and walked back to the front for reentry. This, my friends, was the wrong choice. Upon reaching the front of the building, I was met with another Secret Service agent. I understood and expected this. I explained the situation quickly and mentioned the name of the agent in charge that day, presumably his boss (whom I had *just* been with). I joked and referenced their walkie-talkie system. "Maybe you could radio him and ask him to beam me up, Scotty?" I didn't, I didn't.

He was not amused with me and would not let me in. I showed this man photos on the back of my cameras, taken mere minutes ago of Mr. Donald Trump himself. I was wearing a badge and lanyard that read "TRUMP—Staff Photographer—Gene Ho." But still, there was no explanation he would accept, and he refused to make the call to confirm with anyone else.

So, I said to myself, there's more than one way to get to the Starship. I briskly (and quite heatedly) walked back to where I had exited. I knocked on the window. Secret Service there saw me, knew me, and let me back in. I quickly explained that I had gotten locked out while looking for the fastest route to the stage. Thankfully, they called in to every agent along the maze to promptly get me back to the auditorium moments before Trump took the stage.

Redemption!

I didn't need a babysitter! The head of Secret Service radioed down the line that I was coming through and voila! Boom! I accepted my personal escort with swagger.

Well, then things got a bit more interesting,

I had already lost a little time with Captain Kirk at the front door, so I was in a hurry. I hustled to scout the crowd size. I found my best angle for Trump's entrance, and I settled into position on the left of the main stage. Then, as I waited for Trump to emerge, I felt a tug on my right arm. It was a rather forceful tug that in milliseconds turned into a jerk. Then I was briskly yanked off the stage. As I struggled to compute, I looked over my shoulder and who should I see? It was none other than Secret Service Kirk from the front door.

There were at least three levels of security that I was aware of:

One was the picture in your head: stoic, sharply dressed men in tailored suits, dark sunglasses, and earpiece wires. Like statues, they moved only to speak into their sleeves. They were an unmistakably intimidating force for the protective detail.

While this was never openly made known to me, most of us can guess that there were also the random persons in the crowd—those who appeared to be just the guy from your deli's meat counter but more likely the incognito protection. They were always there. They never watched like the rest. They weren't watching the event or following its cadence. They were watching the watchers.

Then there were the other members of the Secret Service team, the battle-ready squad. They looked like traditional police officers, except they wore all black. They donned full protective gear and had "Secret Service" emblazoned on their bulletproof vest. This was what I imagine must have been the action crew, with muscle and fearlessness.

My thoughts were confirmed. The tap on my shoulder that became a yank off the stage came from him, the battle-ready kind.

It had been his duty to guard one of the entrances, a responsibility he took seriously and intensely. So you can imagine his shock when he looked to the stage and saw *me*. The guy he'd just denied access. Yes, *me*—the camera guy, the obvious assassin, the Chinese one with long hair, blue suede shoes, and *really* bad comedy.

He grabbed me and pulled me to the back.

It was humiliating on so many levels. The obvious reason was this happened moments before Trump took the stage. That meant we had a captive audience. Worse, for me, was that *I'd* become an issue. The agents in the suits had to come in to find out what was holding things up—only to discover it was me. I stood there with my head hung as if prepared for house arrest. I awaited my boot-sized ankle monitor until finally, thankfully, the head Secret Service agent came in and vindicated me.

To this day, I regret being so meek in the situation. I left my voice, and I got bulldozed. I was completely humiliated. This was the one chance I had to speak my mind and call someone out for *his* mistake. I was always being shown mine. This was the one opportunity to decimate all the hoops I was being made to jump through to do my job. This was the one chance I had to set the tone for future events. If I'd had more confidence and made it an issue, I believe I could have changed how the lead advance team viewed me.

But I didn't. I was too afraid to be viewed as a complainer. I was too scared of being fired.

Much of me wishes I had made a big deal about it and fought for my position. Instead, for the rest of the campaign, I was at the mercy of each lead advance. Hindsight being twenty-twenty, perhaps it was the ulterior motives I had.

The goal remained: I wanted to be one of the originals still standing at the campaign's end. I did relinquish the satisfaction of being right in that moment, but in the end, I won. I can't help but think, though, the road would have been a lot smoother had I come unhooked and stood my ground.

Leading me to Abner, a man whose battle cry sounds like that of a Tears for Fears jam:

So these are my schemes
And these are my plans …
When it's all mixed up,
Better break it down …
—"Break It Down Again"

**Meet Abner**

Abner was the cousin of and commander in chief for the king of Israel, King Saul. At that time, the Israelites were battling the Philistines. The Philistines had brought out their biggest soldier, Goliath. Goliath was a Nephilim giant, recorded at standing nine feet. Every warrior in King Saul's army was terrified when Goliath called to them. He sought to fight one-on-one. Not one in King Saul's army was willing to fight the giant.

Then David, a mere fifteen-year-old boy, volunteered to fight. Without wearing protective armor, David took on Goliath. He carried with him a slingshot, five stones, and his faith in God.

David said to the Philistine, "You come against me with the sword and spear and javelin, but I come against you in the name of the Lord Almighty …"
—1 Samuel 17:45

David conquered the giant with the first stone. King Saul and Abner sat in awe, looking upon young David's victory. The king said to Abner, "Whose son is that young man?" (I love this line. Aspire to raise children who succeed at a degree that people wonder, "Whose child is this?")

As it turned out, David was all around a really great guy. The king hired him to play his harp around the castle. David was well liked and earned great respect among the king's people. Eventually Saul became jealous of David's successes. The Israelites would say David's courage led him to conquer tens of thousands while Saul conquered only thousands. This courageous boy defeated their most mighty foe and continued fearlessly into battles for the king. Saul's envy grew.

The battles between those loyal to King Saul and those loyal to David went on for years. It became King Saul's consuming preoccupation to have David killed. Saul's evil plotting and growing obsession with destroying David even caused the king to lose the adoration of his own son, Jonathan.

Abner continued as the commander in chief of Saul's army. King Saul and his army went into battle yet again with the Philistine army. This time the Philistines would prevail. The Philistines not only slaughtered much of the Israelite army, but they also killed three of Saul's sons.

As they closed in on the king, Saul became critically wounded. There was no escaping. The only person left with him was his shield bearer. King Saul asked his shield bearer to kill him, knowing it would be better to die quickly at the hand of his servant than whatever the Philistines would have in store for him. His shield bearer was too afraid and refused to kill the king. At that, Saul fell on his own sword, taking his life.

With the king dead, a civil war erupted. On one side, there was David, who was pronounced the king of Judah (the south). As commander in chief, Abner put his support behind Ishbaal, the only remaining son of Saul. With the authority to do so, Abner named Ishbaal as the king of Israel (the north).

Not long after, Abner became involved with one of Saul's concubines. Maybe it was love, or maybe it was politically driven. At the time, taking the deceased king's concubine could be considered a display of power. Whatever the motivation, Ishbaal wasn't very happy with Abner, and he brought it up to him.

It was then that Abner flew into a rage:

> Abner was very angry because of what Ishbaal said and he answered, "Am I a dog's head—on Judah's side? This very day I am loyal to the house of your father Saul and to his family and friends. I haven't handed you over to David. Yet now you accuse me of an offense involving this woman."
>
> —2 Samuel 3:8

His frustration was defensible. Abner had been loyal to the king in virtually every way. He'd probably repressed his desire for this woman for years. Now, with his cousin Saul dead, he was free to take her as his wife.

More than anything Abner was angry with his thankless nephew. Ishbaal had been seated as the new king because Abner had given him the title. With Abner's influence over the people, he had suggested Ishbaal as Saul's replacement. Now Ishbaal had the nerve to chastise him for making a relationship with this woman? Abner was livid and became so enraged that Ishbaal was terrified of him.

Abner had always been a man of the people and had great influence. He had been gaining strength in the kingdom. Meanwhile the territory was growing weaker under the poor guidance of Ishbaal. After the fallout, Abner secretly sent his messengers to David's kingdom to broker a deal. Because of the divide between the kingdoms, if Abner had shown up himself, he probably would have been killed on the spot. So Abner sent his representatives to negotiate with David. Abner offered to rally the people and show his support for David in order to overtake the reign of Ishbaal, turning over the kingdom of Israel to David.

And this joining of forces ushered King David into power.

Abner lived life on a political roller coaster. But one thing remained constant: his ability to maintain a position of power. He watched young David destroy the giant. Abner knew then that David had God's favor. Yet he remained loyal to his cousin, Saul, to the end of his days.

Abner lived by his wits and generally acted according to what was best for him. He may have lived with questionable principles, but when it came time to choose sides, he did so with conviction.

Sometimes it's ulterior motives that alter the course of history. One of the great catalysts for change in the story of Abner just happens to be unleashing his tongue.

**Enter Trump**

Trump built his reputation as a no-nonsense business tycoon. While some of his ferocity was genuine, it would seem he often used it as a powerful business tool.

Consider the funniest person you know personally—that friend who inevitably has you in stitches when you're together. Then ask yourself how that person would fare in public speaking, or even as a stand-up comedian. It doesn't always translate. I have friends who are hilarious over beers in the backyard, but it doesn't mean they could be successful stand-up comedians. Luckily, neither do they desire to be.

My longtime friend, Richie Minervini, is a professional comedian. Richie is known as the "godfather" of stand-up comedy. In the 1980s he ran East Side Comedy Club in Long Island, New York. It was there that many of the household names we now know as kings of comedy honed their skills. Richie's club gave career beginnings to budding comics like Eddie Murphy, Jerry Seinfeld, Kevin James, and Jim Carrey. Even Trump's nemesis Rosie O'Donnell grew up not far from Minervini's club and made her debut on East Side's stage.

Also working at Minervini's club in the '80s: yours truly. It wasn't for my entertainment value if you can believe it; I was the dishwasher. As a high school youth, night after night I would soak up the acts and study stage performance and delivery. In the presence of greats both on and off stage, one aspect rang true: most of these comedians weren't 24-7 funny guys. While socializing over dinner, it's not as though it's a series of endless gut-busting one-liners. Yet when they took to the stage, hilarity ensued.

My point is the aspects of a person we see publicly, aspects that define his or her character, don't represent the whole person. In the words of William Shakespeare, "All the world's a stage."

Years later, while on stage in one of Trump's Atlantic City casinos, Richie Minervini was performing his stand-up act. As it would happen, Trump was a member of his audience. Taking the opportunity for comedy gold, Richie made a few pokes at the easy target. After a live, unscripted back-and-forth with Donald Trump, Richie slugged the final one-liner. "After this roast, I suppose I can expect to find out if the rumors are true when I don't get paid." As expected, the crowd erupted in laughter.

We believe we know the pieces that make up a man we've never had an exchange with—until we do. As Richie tells it, not only was he paid for his employment, but Trump also had seen to it that Richie was paid double!

Trump is a wily man. He masterfully created an image for himself, and he is skilled at using the idea people have of him to his advantage. He uses irritability and anger effectively as a motivational tool. I've seen him very upset before, and it was authentic. Anger and passion come from the same place. To care for something enough to fight for it is exactly the type of person we should hope for to run the country. Just as a comedian can keep a room rolling for an hour set, it's merely a fraction of the whole. For as many times as I saw Trump's intensity, I also saw his sensitivity.

It was November 24, 2015, just two days before Thanksgiving. Trump was holding a rally in my hometown of Myrtle Beach. This event was particularly special since it was one of the first events where he had brought his family with him. I'm sure it was in part convenience as they made their way south to Mar-a-Lago for the holiday together. It was on this day I met Melania, Ivanka, and Tiffany for the first time. I also was honored to meet Trump's youngest son, Barron.

Like Trump, I like to sandwich in business with pleasure. The last few years I've taken my family to Disney World, and while there I'll take an evening off to speak to the Orlando Camera Club. The kids come along while I speak to the crowd. I think it gives a valuable insight to what I do for a living. It gives them an appreciation for this profession, which affords us the pleasure of enjoying the vacation time. Barron reminded me a lot of my son Barry in that he's not *always* thrilled to hear me speak, nor is he *exactly* impressed.

On this day, it seemed that was how Barron Trump felt. He was just nine years old, so you can imagine a political rally was not his first choice for how to spend his holiday vacation. I could see Trump sensed his youngest son wasn't exactly stoked to be there.

Prior to joining the VIP room for photos, Trump and family were given a room to settle into as their home base. In this room was a table with various items that our local coordinators were hopeful Trump might autograph. There was everything from "Trump" MAGA hats and copies of *The Art of the Deal* to personal memorabilia.

There was also a second table, which contained various gifts for Trump from supporters. The gift table was always the quirkiest collection of items. Normally it was filled with handmade sketches, letters, and artwork. Supporters loved to give Trump gifts. Children would give him mini Lego figures they'd made to look like him. Artists would gift hand-painted portraits of Trump. It was a unique way for individuals to share a piece of themselves with him. This day brought one such uncommon gift.

A local gun maker had handcrafted a personalized rifle for Trump. I will never forget it. He opened the case, spying the brilliant attention to detail, and said, "Barron, come here! You have *got* to check this thing out!" As a dad myself, I knew he was taking that quiet opportunity in the chaos of it all to share a one-on-one moment with his son. It was a side of him we don't get to see: the tenderness, enthusiasm, and joy in Donald Trump, the father.

We shouldn't need access to those pieces of him to know they're there.

• • • • • • • • • • • • • • • • • • • • • • • • • • • • • • • • • • • • • • • • • • • • • • • • • • • •

I can wholeheartedly attest that Donald Trump is wildly charming in person. I remember meeting him for the first time, unsure of what to expect. Admittedly, it's hard not to let the preconceived idea of what you've seen on TV swish around in your brain.

I've photographed numerous celebrities in the past; some are beloved by the public, but in private they're insufferable. I can tell you with conviction: Trump in person is cordial and gracious, and he has quite a sense of humor.

One of the first times I worked with him, a staff member from the hotel approached us backstage. The man asked Trump if he would yell, "You're fired" so he might record it on his cell phone. I was sure Trump would say no. I was wrong. Not only did Trump happily play along, but he also asked for the man's name. Trump even did two takes and named him personally as he bellowed, "You're fired!"

At the time, I imagined what I would do with that same audio/video clip! I imagined all the hilarious ways I could spin a promo with Donald Trump hollering, "Gene Ho, you're fired."

I didn't want to be fired, of course. For me, there was an end-game wish. If Mr. Trump was truly considering a run for president, I wanted to be there for the ride. As the months carried on, it became clear: he was really doing it. And so was I.

He was certainly the underdog when it came to the presidential race. Compared to others, he didn't have decades of time spent in political office—although for many supporters that was a positive rather than a negative. Trump's passion and charisma were impossible to ignore, and they made up the difference.

The media reported tirelessly each time he said anything that could be spun even remotely controversial. In no time, he owned the airwaves. Meanwhile anyone in attendance at these rallies could see and hear it for themselves. There was a clear difference between the live version and what the nation watched later. The words he spoke were pieced together, torn out of context, and bent to sell the headlines that painted him as a loose cannon.

Trump-mania consumed the nation.

When it came time for the first primary race in February 2016, Trump was projected to be the winner. The Iowa Caucus takes the torch and leads the nation. Sweet Midwestern Iowa is a very interesting state when it comes to politics. It is the first gauge in national politics. Iowa isn't particularly large or overwhelmingly wealthy, but the state proudly maintains the title as first. As first, Iowa helps to filter out the candidates who are unable to form a strong campaign following.

Iowa demands something different. Its winner usually has spent a lot of time in the state, boots on the ground. They have invested one-on-one time—at parades, cafes, and pancake breakfasts, and going door-to-door.

Mr. Trump marched to his own beat. He didn't do all those things in mass like his competition. For some, he used a once-in-a-lifetime approach like the day he showed up at the Iowa State Fair with his helicopter and gave rides. Due to his unusually large following, his campaign found more pack for the punch with large-scale rallies than down-the-street diners. While Trump didn't run a traditional Iowa campaign, he was projected to win.

He didn't.

In many ways, it was an embarrassment for Trump. He is a man set out to win. Bigly. At that point, I'd spent over a year in his presence, and I had never seen his wrath. That was about to change. The first event I worked after the Iowa loss stands in the record books of my mind.

Trump took the stage and spoke brilliantly before the crowd. His speech was upbeat and inspired. Those in attendance who'd watched the rally talk would have no idea how livid he was.

When we went backstage, Trump called up one of the higher-level staffers for an impromptu meeting. They sought out a room for privacy. After a brief exchange, they emerged from the room. It was clear that he was not happy.

We were all on edge, waiting. Trump called a couple of other team members to his attention. It was then that he unloaded. I have never in my life seen someone get bawled out so badly. To be clear, there was no cussing, and nothing inappropriate was said or done. This was a dressing down like I have never seen before. What made it worse for the receivers was the fact that there were upwards of twenty people in the room.

Once Trump had finished, everyone in the room was like a guilty dog that couldn't look the Alpha in the eye. As he left the room, he addressed the rest of us, saying sharply, "Just get the job done."

We got the message loud and clear, and we did just that. Later that month, Trump went on to win the New Hampshire and South Carolina primaries.

We saw Trump's rage that day, and it empowered us to do more and to do it better. For as much as he was there to reward the right decisions, he also made it clear he would not accept the wrong ones. He had given us instruction and a good dose of fear to take with it. Motivation through fear is the core of being alive in the fight to survive.

Much like Abner gained the respect of the kingdom's followers through the fear of his tongue-lashing, Trump, too, earned support and saw results by knowing when to verbally strike!

By far, my best friend on the campaign trail:
Pastor Mark Burns.
Mark was the "warm-up show" at many of the Trump rallies.

There was a lot of hurry up & wait on the campaign trail.
This gave us the opportunity to spend time backstage,
catching up on what's good in life.

On this day, Trump needed a witness
as he signed the legal document
to have his name listed on the "ticket"
for a Republican Primary Election.

A man well versed in signing the dotted line...

Not only did I witness for him as he signed,
but he also observed closely as I authorized
the documents.

I stunt doubled on this day, as his photographer
and as his official Notary Public.

The story my future grandchildren will tell about this epic
moment is perhaps somewhat different from how it really happened...

The real story included a phone call to my wife, in which
I gasped my way through dry heaves to explain to her that there
wasn't a Notary in the house.

This, followed by me speed-walking through the parking lot
to my trunk, where my notary stamp waited to save the day.

As a wedding photographer, I had carried the title of Notary Public;
for those 'just in case' moments when an officiant couldn't make it.
I never could have known my 'just in case' might cover
our Presidential history as well.

# Chapter 6

### Joshua—The Pragmatic Principal

Bring the woman out with all who belong to her, as you swore to her that you would do. The young men who had been spies went and brought Rahab out, with her father and mother and brothers and all who belonged to her.
—Joshua 6:22, 23

My first real job was an internship with a newspaper. This was the early 1990s, well before the days of the internet. Back then news was sourced primarily via the evening broadcast and newsprint. Following the internship, I started as a reporter for the *Sun News* in Myrtle Beach. It was a respected position, and the paper had a large readership.

One of the first stories I reported on was a local high school football game. As a young reporter, I took great pride in my work. I created a strategy: I would report on the game as if I were at a Super Bowl and later describe it to my roommate.

Back then, of course, there were no instant news outlets. No online news, social media, blogs, cell calls, or texting. After the game, those in attendance would know the outcome. For everyone else, unless the local television station reported it, there was no way to know who won. It was the local newspaper that kept everyone in the know.

On a crisp Friday night in autumn, I went to the game and soaked in every aspect of being there. I went back to the newsroom and wrote a story that would make readers feel like they were in the stands: the smells of popcorn and turf, the rowdy fans screaming their competitive banter, the adrenaline in the air. For every run and fumble, I told the story of an epic back-and-forth. I was so proud of this piece.

That night, once completed, I submitted the story to my editor. It was then that my editor proclaimed, "Wow, nice job! Just one thing, Ho: What was the score?"

I had explained everything in brilliant detail, but the single most important aspect I had completely forgotten to report. My editor calmly told me it was no big deal. "Just go back and check your notes," he said.

Shamefully, not only had I not written it in my notes, but I also hadn't kept notes at all. I hadn't even thought about notes. I didn't think I needed them. I lived that game and soaked up every facet of being there. In a sea of well-crafted details, I had completely overlooked the obvious.

Details are worthless without keeping score.

Ironically, exactly the opposite can also be true: Keeping score is worthless without the details. A great story without the score is worth nothing, just as a score with no details is nothing more than two numbers at the bottom of the ESPN television screen.

Details and scores go hand in hand. I'm the kind of person who doesn't always keep score. That can be a good thing, to be the kind of person who really lives in the moment. But ultimately keeping score is a necessity. It keeps track of winners and losers. It tracks who you owe and who owes you.

When my daughter, Luna, turned four, she desperately wanted to be a dancer. So I asked her if she wanted to take gymnastics or a dance class. A lady ahead of her time, she opted for both. I found a suitable place for her. She was so young. While I wanted to be accommodating to my aspiring little peanut, I was realistic about schedules. I signed her up for classes at the gymnastics studio closest to me.

All was well in the world, and my daughter enjoyed herself. At the end of the first semester, one of the instructors approached me at the recital. She mentioned how nice it was that I had my daughter attend their school—despite everything that had happened.

At first, I was dumbfounded. What had happened? What was she talking about? I thought hard about it. Then I remembered. Twenty-five years earlier, when my photography career began, I wasn't taking pictures of celebrities, and I certainly wasn't taking pictures of presidential candidates. I was making a living taking portraits of children at dance and gymnastic schools.

At one time in my career, I held accounts with almost every dance and gymnastic school in the area. The divorce from my first wife set off a chain reaction of implosions within my business accounts. She had been the point of contact, and she took the photos at many of these establishments.

A large portion of these schools insisted on keeping their personal photographer. They stuck with her in the split. It was virtually overnight that I lost every school account I'd had. I watched my hard work disintegrate before my eyes. As you can imagine, this didn't sit well with me. I was quite upset. I made my position known with many of the withdrawn business owners. I insisted if their loyalty were not with me, I was sure to never do business with them again.

Standing there, staring at the proud face of my curly headed little girl on the balance beam, I realized I had completely forgotten. I hadn't remembered to hate them. I hadn't kept score. I didn't spend years pining away and plotting. I kept living. After the dissolution of the dance-school era, I transitioned my studio from school portrait photography to high-end weddings.

Beyond that—somewhere amid a sea of the most beautiful ceremonies on the southern East Coast—I had also managed to find my way in as Donald Trump's campaign photographer. Without realizing it, not only had I let go, but I also was better for it.

After this realization, I stood conflicted. If I had so easily forgotten the score of the bad, how many times had I forgotten to keep score of the good?

If someone has done right by me, do I acknowledge that act? Do I remember that good deed five years down the road? Fifteen years later? More importantly, have I repaid the good?

I bring to you the story of Joshua, a righteous leader with a profound knack for getting to the core of a situation. Joshua was a man who lived by the Book of Law and never failed to keep score.

**Meet Joshua**

Joshua was the right-hand man of Moses. After Moses's death, Joshua was asked to lead the Israelites. Joshua was special. He was one of only two men who escaped the rule of Egypt and lived to set foot in the Promised Land.

In the Bible, there are several people who received God's blessing of something special. Joshua was given the gift of invincibility in battle. When Joshua charged into battle, he was guaranteed victory on the condition that he kept to God's law. He would meditate on the words night and day, and he was expected to never deviate from them. This gives us some insight into why minute details were relevant for Joshua. God stressed to him the importance of obeying everything written in the Book of Law.

It was fitting that a man focused on details and specifics would create techniques and routines to remain orderly. After the nation of Israel crossed the Jordan River, Joshua ordered his men to pull twelve stones from the bare floor of the river. With these stones they created a riverside marker, noting the event. Each of the twelve stones represented a tribe of Israel. It was said that it should be a sign for their children, a reminder to tell them how God separated the waters of the Jordan that day.

Joshua was big on landmarks, placeholders, and markers. Markers helped retain significance and provide something tangible to see and touch. Marking the event made the reference for memory greater—like a souvenir from a family vacation draws up memories to be shared again and again.

Another impressive account of Joshua's use of markers involved a simple scarlet cord. Joshua prepared to take possession of the city of Jericho. Before invading Jericho, he sent two scouts into the city. As word spread that there were spies among them, the king of Jericho set out to search for them. A woman named Rahab had taken the spies into her home. The king sought her out and demanded she reveal their location. She sent the town's men on a wild chase when she insisted the spies had left earlier. Meanwhile Joshua's spies were, in fact, on her rooftop, hidden from capture. It was an incredibly brave thing to have done. Had the king known of her deceit, she surely would have been killed.

In exchange for her protection, Rahab and the spies made an agreement. In appreciation the spies vowed that when Joshua and his men invaded the city, they would spare Rahab and her family. The marker was in one small detail. Rahab would hang a scarlet cord in her window. With this symbol the men would be able to identify her home. Their promise to her was that anyone in her home would be safe when Joshua's men came.

As promised, when Joshua invaded the city, Rahab and her family were spared:

> Joshua said to the two men who had scouted the land, "Go to the prostitute's house and bring the woman out of there, and all who are with her, just as you promised her."
>
> —Joshua 6:22

Yes, Rahab was a prostitute—some may say an unlikely candidate to be used by God. We are faced yet again with the reminder that God does some of his finest work through outcast material. Regardless of her social standing, at the core Rahab was an honorable person. Through her God-fearing belief, she saved not only her own life but the lives of her family as well. The lesson is in the smallest detail: the scarlet cord.

In a curious spell, I estimated the length of time between the exchange with Rahab and Joshua's invasion. A deal was brokered and a scarlet cord hung (chapter 2), and then seemingly the next day an invasion occurred (chapter 6). At a quick glance, it would seem simple enough to calculate.

As you can imagine, it wasn't *quite* that simple. We are living in the twenty-first century, quite accustomed to the "now" era, but things were not so swift in the Bronze Age.

I calculated the distance and time it would have taken for the spies to travel back from Jericho after meeting Rahab. Then I added the time it would have taken the nation of Israel to cross the Jordan. Their population would have easily exceeded a million. To cross the river Jordan, I estimated to be the length of their month of Nisan. Following the river crossing, Joshua assembled the twelve men to erect the memorial stones at the Jordan. Chapter 5 of Joshua notes another celebration of Passover. All things considered, I estimate that from the time Rahab made the deal to the time they were invaded would be about one year.

Imagine for a moment how much trust it required for this story line to play out like it did. Rahab had hidden enemy spies in her home. Then she lied to the king about it. While living among them, she waited for one year to be saved from those whom she'd deceived. Perhaps over time it got easier, but consider those first few days and weeks. The king's goons likely visited her relentlessly, believing she knew something more about the men she'd seen. Even her neighbors had likely probed for details. Still, she kept her story straight. She waited. Rahab had faith. The scarlet cord, the secret symbol of her hopeful salvation, hung in wait of her allies … for one year.

Her faith was well placed. Joshua not only had a great memory, but he was a man of his word. Joshua's attention to detail and his ability to keep score stood against the chaos of battle and time. To add to his character, Joshua overcame great trials. In all his years, he never had a steady home. His entire life was spent traveling to find peace. He was born in Egypt as a slave, spent forty years roaming the desert, and spent the remainder of his life fighting for liberty.

Through it all, Joshua kept a running track record of the good. In this instance, when Rahab saved the lives of Joshua's spies, he remembered. All things balanced, there was a time when Joshua also kept score of the bad. This was true in the story of Achan.

After the scarlet cord and the fall of Jericho, Joshua sent his men on to the next conquest, the city of Ai. The seemingly invincible Joshua fully expected a victory. That was understandable since he and his soldiers had overcome everyone they had battled. Confidently, Joshua sent a mere three-thousand-man infantry to take down Ai. Not only was he unsuccessful, but also thirty-six of Joshua's men were killed in the attempt.

The defeat at Ai was not only an embarrassment to him but an emotional upheaval as well. The widows and mothers of the men killed were left writhing in pain, and Joshua knew it was on his charge that they were lost.

The scriptures clearly paint the picture of a man suffering great emotional turmoil. Remember Joshua not as a character in the Bible but as a man suffering great depression and living regret. Upon hearing of the loss, Joshua strained to tear the clothing from his body and lay immobilized in the dust for hours. Finally, when he came to speak, he could only cry out fearfully, "Why?"

I find it telling that the Bible mentions specifically thirty-six casualties. It does not state three thousand soldiers went in and *some* did not return. Thirty-six men were lost that day. The hard numbers serve to note the harsh realism of what had happened. It helped convey how unaccustomed they were to loss. The impact of every individual was felt and accounted for.

In time, all things come to light. There was an explanation for their unexpected loss. They had retributions to pay for the actions of one deceitful sinner among them, a man named Achan. Joshua's army had been instructed not to keep anything they found in their takeover of a city. However, in the raid of Jericho, Achan had intentionally disobeyed orders. He had stolen and hidden riches for himself. We see the consequence of his actions, how one man's mistake caused immediate misfortune for those around him. He intentionally defied God's command. As a result, God's protection was compromised, and the lives of thirty-six Israelites were lost.

Joshua kept score.

At the Lord's request, Joshua set out to learn who had disobeyed the word of the Lord. Tribe by tribe, clan by clan, the men stood before Joshua until it came to Achan. With no reservation, he showed immediate regret and confessed. While Joshua remembered and rewarded those who had done right, he was equally ruthless in administering justice against those who brought harm to his people. Despite Achan's remorse and willful confession, it was ordered that he, along with his family, be put to death.

In the wake of the Old Testament's "an eye for an eye" and in keeping score, Joshua repaid the righteous with good as often as he repaid the unjust with its rightful share. We've watched Mr. Trump utilize the same approach. For as much as we've seen him publicly lash out at the unjust, he is first to praise the benevolent.

**Enter Trump**

In an interview Donald Trump gave to New York–based radio personality Bob Lonsberry in April 2016, Trump was asked if he had a favorite Bible passage that helped shape his character in life. He replied, "An eye for an eye. That's not a particularly nice thing … we can learn a lot from the Bible."

There are many references in the Bible to an eye for an eye, but the most commonly known is from Exodus:

> But if there is serious injury, you are to take life for life, eye for eye,
> tooth for tooth, hand for hand, foot for foot, burn for burn,
> wound for wound, bruise for bruise.
> —Exodus 21:23–25

Later it was Jesus who rebuked this, saying not to resist an evil person. "Should your enemy walk a mile, you walk with them two miles." In so many words, Jesus instructs us gently to "kill your enemy with kindness." Jesus asks us to live more compassionately and more forgivingly than those before Him. This doesn't erase the lessons to be learned through the vengeance of the Lord seen in the Old Testament. Still, there are many instances throughout the book of John where Jesus asks us to take the high road. In Romans, we learn the score will be settled by the Lord, our Father:

> Do not take revenge, my dear friends, but leave room for God's wrath,
> for it is written:

"It is mine to avenge; I will repay," says the Lord.

On the contrary: If your enemy is hungry, feed him; if he is thirsty, give him something to drink. In doing this, you will heap burning coals on his head.
—Romans 12:19–20

The first one-on-one conversation I held with Donald Trump was in January 2015 on board his private jet. I was excited; I had been a huge fan for years, and I'd read all his books. I took the opportunity to prove my fandom by recalling my favorite mentions in *The Art of the Deal*. I shared how he had inspired me in business and noted how I'd particularly loved one lesson, as it related to my own experiences.

Trump was a builder. I am a photographer. While these are two vastly different professions, there was one thing we had in common: perspective. In *The Art of the Deal*, Trump explained how he approached one of his job sites. Immediately he could see the building was off by a couple of degrees.

As a photographer, I pride my photos on having "perfect nineties." What that means is right angles are right; my subject and the background shouldn't be (unintentionally) askew. A crooked building is imperfect just as an improperly composed photo is flawed.

Quick to make a joke, he jabbed, "See, I told you. Attention to detail! I suppose now you owe me twenty percent of your earnings." Trump laughed. There was no shortage of stories from those, like me, who had a personal account to share.

As a billionaire, made in business, Trump has had plenty of individuals who were seeking face-to-face time to pitch their proposals. One such individual showed me a rejection letter he'd received from Trump's organization. I presume (for posterity's sake) he sought to have it signed as a memento from the presidential hopeful. The letter he had previously received from Trump's review board stated something to the effect that while they appreciated the offer, they were not interested. The primary factor at issue was that the proposal was "out of Mr. Trump's area of expertise."

I can appreciate that phrase. Business is about the details. It's about how well you know the trade and how effectively you've mastered the details of it. It's also about being honest when something is out of your strong suit.

A few years ago, I decided I was going to take my entrepreneurial spirit and get into flipping houses. I started small with a little condo. It couldn't be that hard, I thought. They do it on HGTV. Buy a home, fix it up, and sell it for more that you paid for it. It sounded easy enough. Everything went as I had planned, except for one little detail at closing: 6 percent. While 6 percent doesn't sound like a lot, if you didn't factor it from the front, 6 percent is huge.

In a new business venture, with my inexperience and naivety, I didn't calculate the eventual fee from the real estate company that sold and closed the property. I was so tied up in the minute details that I'd forgotten the big picture. What a huge difference just a few percentage points made.

After the electrician, the painter, and the carpenter had been paid, and after new appliances, a few windows and fixtures, I had about $6,000 left. It was just enough to pay the real estate agent. Those who'd mastered the details made money. I did not as I had not.

Always pay attention to detail.

Later that year, I was asked to witness history and detail it. Literally. For this I will forever appreciate the importance of mastering my craft and owning the details. This is the story I lived:

It was September 2015, and Mr. Trump was in Columbia, South Carolina. He was filing the declaration that would allow his name on the state Republican ballot for the primary election. It was on this day that I was asked to be the official witness of Trump's signature as a South Carolina notary public.

The story as (I dream) it happened is as follows: Mr. Trump calmly surveyed the room. He stopped intermittently, pausing on the many reputable faces from his most beloved inner circle. He nodded from time to time as though to acknowledge their importance. Finally, he settled on my face, narrowed his eyes, and after a deep inhale, said aloud, "Who other than my dearest old friend, Gene Ho, to witness my signature on this monumental document?"

Well, it wasn't *quite* like that. Although, as stories go, one day my great-grandchildren may tell it something like that. Being nominated for the role wasn't quite as epic a tale.

The day offered a rather small-scale event. The idea that it was no big deal may explain why one of the tiniest details was accidentally overlooked. The person coordinating the event had forgotten to arrange a notary to legalize the momentous moment. There before me, standing arm's length away, stood the one and only Mr. Donald Trump in need of an official South Carolina notary public. As fate would have it, I was a notary public.

I carry my stamp with me everywhere. It's a habit I've adopted as a longtime wedding photographer. Experience had faced me with the "stuck-in-traffic officiant" more than once. I sought the ability to say, "Your uncle can stand in to read the vows if you like; we have the option to move on." As a notary, I've been able to sign off on the marriage certificate. The show goes on. No hiccups, no drama, and no tears equal one happy (married) couple. It's one of the many wedding-day perks I offer.

Once the Trump team began to breathe again, they arranged for me to sign. With my stamp and seal in hand, I joined the room, cameras still slung on each shoulder. I had to focus all my energies not to throw up as the nerves bubbled. Trump looked to me, dumbfounded, then traced back to the rest of our crew and said with a snicker, "This is the guy?"

We watched firsthand as Trump crossed the t's. After I'd witnessed Trump's signature, he passed the pen to me and waited. He personally watched me sign and finalize the document. It was yet another concentrated act of his patience and thorough attention to detail.

While Trump was big on details, he was also about keeping score. He had a memory like a steel trap. I first realized that Trump had no problem keeping score on transgressions at an event for which he was holding a private news conference. Maybe *private* is better said as *impromptu*.

On this day, Trump arrived at a campaign luncheon. Without forewarning, he allowed a handful of the reporters present to question him. There couldn't have been but five or six reporters in the room. This would have been an incredible opportunity from a journalism standpoint. Trump headlines had ruled the media since he announced his run.

It seemed almost immediately that Mr. Trump recognized the reporter holding court. In opening, the reporter noted that he was from CNN. I can't quote the exact question posed, but it regarded the release of his economic plan. Trump calmly replied, "Yes, I will release the plan, but it will certainly not be with you."

****

Trump then and Trump now has had a love/hate relationship with the mainstream media. I watched him on the campaign trail so unbelievably respectful and kind to so many, but it was clear in that moment he had a bone to pick. He appeared he was out to right a past wrong, with either this reporter specifically or CNN in general. His delivery was slow and wry, with a classic comedic value. Everyone in the room had a quiet giggle—except for the man from CNN.

Trump also kept score when it came to the good, and he remembered those who loyally stood with him. Early in the campaign, Trump didn't garner much support from the Republican establishment. While the political endorsements swirled with representatives backing their respective candidate, Trump initially wasn't on the receiving end. Finally, on January 27, 2016, at a rally in Gilbert, South Carolina, the lieutenant governor from South Carolina, Henry McMaster, stepped up and publicly declared his support for Mr. Trump. Since it is one of the first states to vote, South Carolina has the power of influence when it comes to the Republican primary. At the time, McMaster was the highest-ranking South Carolina politician to endorse Donald Trump. Henry McMaster broke with the ranks of the established Republicans and joined Trump on the campaign trail.

After the official announcement, we were at an event with many powerful South Carolina officials in attendance. When Trump found out his initial supporter was there, he insisted McMaster be at his side. "We need the governor here with us," Trump said hopefully. "Well, he's not governor yet, but he will be."

During the campaign, one of Trump's loudest critics was the popular governor of South Carolina, Nikki Haley. She was a well-respected, conservative leader in the state. In turn, her approval or disapproval certainly held weight with the people of South Carolina. Just weeks after McMaster endorsed Mr. Trump, Haley voiced her backing for the Republican establishment's Marco Rubio.

Haley and Trump had their share of public disagreements. Many were surprised when shortly after Trump became president, he appointed Nikki Haley as US ambassador to the United Nations. After all, Trump and Haley had bumped heads during the campaign, and quite publicly so. For many who knew her, Haley made perfect sense for the appointment. She is a dynamic leader. Much to Mr. Trump's credit, he will do what he feels is right, even if it means something is difficult. Even if that means working shoulder to shoulder with someone he doesn't agree with on all points. Nikki Haley is a fighter and diverse in her thinking. She was an incredible choice for the position. Upon accepting the position as UN ambassador, Haley left the governor's post and Lieutenant Governor McMaster ascended to the governorship.

Trump kept the details and the score, much like Joshua.

We can learn from and utilize the core of what Joshua's lesson teaches. Keep a running tab on the good and bad we live daily. The details and the score both count, equally. We have the ability, through chosen actions, to affect the outcome of both in our lives. We are granted authority over the actions of one. Lead the game you desire.

While we benefit in noting wrongs, it is imperative to continue living well. Dredging up only the bad is a stalemate, just as only acknowledging good leaves us vulnerable. Life is a balance.

For your own sake, continue to move forward. Continue to spin good into the world. You weave your own day, control your own actions. What you put out into the world will come back. Choose to play the game well.

If you can't fly, then run.
If you can't run, then walk.
If you can't walk, then crawl.
But whatever you do,
You have to keep moving forward.
—Martin Luther King Jr.

There was no end to the various locations Trump would pack the house.
Rallies were held in retired Navy ships, theaters,
convention centers, farms and stadiums, to name a few.

Trump never knew where he would be from one event to the next.
At a venue where rodeos are held, with comedic delivery
he took the mic with, "Sooo... What kind of place is *this*?"

They say children are a mirror reflecting their parents.

Even if he didn't win the Presidency, Donald Trump would have still been a wildly successful man.

His children are the proof of this.

The Trump children and families are absolutely incredible people.

Lara spent a lot of time on the campaign trail. She did a lot of campaigning, independent of the Donald Trump appearances. She spent a good deal of energy in swing states working to champion 'Women for Trump.'

Jared & Ivanka were expecting their third child through the campaign. Still, Ivanka made numerous appearances in support of her dad.

# Chapter 7

### Mephibosheth—The Master Presenter

Mephibosheth, Saul's grandson, also went down to meet the king. He had not taken care of his feet or trimmed his mustache or washed his clothes from the day the king left until the day he returned safely.
—2 Samuel 19:24

My mom gave me a bit of advice years ago. "Eugene," she said, "it's much better to pretend you're poor when you're rich than to pretend you are rich when you are poor." The obvious lesson in this advice is that of humility. It also touches on the importance of showmanship and the value of how you present yourself to others. Ultimately whether you have or you have not doesn't encompass who you are as much as what you carry into the world.

Not long after my mother shared this gem with me, I was having dinner with a few colleagues and potential hires. I was able to see just what she meant. It was a small group, a collective meeting of the minds over a simple dinner. One of the young men in the group (let's call him Larry) I had known for years. He was a millennial, just starting out in life. Privately he'd made me aware of his seemingly insurmountable credit card debt and college loans. He was in the torrential bobber-in-the-water part of life when the better half of it feels underwater. Simply put, he wasn't exactly living the high life.

When our waiter approached the table, Larry sat thumbing through the menu, never lifting his eyes to meet the young waiter's gaze.

"Welcome, gentlemen. Can I start you off with some appetizers?"

Larry cut in with a short snarl, "Water."

Completely embarrassed, I first picked my jaw up off the floor. Then I looked to our server. "Yes, water would be great! Thank you." That's when I recognized him. And I'm sure he recognized me.

I knew this young man's parents. His family had *a lot* of money. He didn't need to be waiting tables. In fact, if I had to guess, his father had probably insisted that he get some real-world experience. What better way to understand the value of a dollar than working a minimum-wage position in the service industry, especially with customers like Larry. Whatever the reason, this young waiter had a net worth that surpassed those to whom he was serving blooming onions.

As the dining experience continued, Larry's sad power trip became glaringly obvious. He was taking pleasure in barking orders, showing a full display of his character. Everyone was aware how crude it was (except Larry). It wasn't long before a sort of bond developed between the waiter and the rest of us.

"Sir, what would you like for your entrée?"

"Steak. Medium. And more water," Larry barbed as he spun the menu over the table, back to his "lowly servant."

"And you, sir?"

As he turned to me, we now connected to a higher consciousness. We each knew exactly what the other was thinking and sealed it with a nod and a brow raise. At each condescending Mr. Big Time remark, we exchanged winks around the table. The joke was on Larry. At the end of the night, I thanked our waiter and left him a healthy tip for being part of the show. He'd more than earned it. In case you were wondering, Larry didn't get the job.

In life, presentation can either work for you or against you.

The entire existence of my career is based on the idea of presentation. A wedding is a live production, with no do-overs or dress rehearsals. The décor, the cake, the hair and makeup, the paperwork and costumes, the bridesmaids and shoes, all preserved with live, full-coverage film crews. I go in to a wedding knowing I can win or lose the approval of my client based on my presentation that day. They have hired me for the body of work they trust, but they also hire me truly believing I can deliver an experience.

A close friend of my wife's, Casey Jadge, works as the director of sales at a multimillion-dollar wedding venue. Now, *she* has mastered the art of presentation. Our lifeblood is primarily focused on catering to a couple who are celebrating the fanfare and magic of the biggest day of their life. It might seem commonsensical, but we don't compete for attention since our paycheck is provided by a bride! Casey is a beautiful woman, and she knows how to rein it in.

For weddings, she dresses conservatively; wears square, tortoise-shell glasses; and pulls her hair back in a neat bun. The message conveyed is simple but clear: "In all the land, no one is more fair than the lady in white."

Another great example of presentation in my field is lens selection. Some portrait photographers love to make a show. They haul massively long lenses and expensive-looking gear. They bring these items as if trying to say, "Don't question my skills. Look at this gargantuan lens! *Obviously* with a lens like this, I'm a very good photographer!"

When I take pictures, simplicity is key. It's not any kind of marketing play. It's about function. I've found that for portraiture, a good 85 mm fixed lens does the trick. It's not a terribly flashy lens. The purpose of a good lens isn't what you see by observing the lens; it's what the lens "sees" that counts.

In so many words, I'm saying that when I'm out shooting, I don't look like a professional photographer. On more than one occasion, I've been out working and stumbled across the helpful "Uncle Bob." Looking like an amateur with my modest lens, I've been offered more than my fair share of tips of the trade. I love playing along, intently listening to the learned photographer offering instruction on angles and lighting.

Presentation is one of the most basic things we have authority over in our daily lives. How you carry yourself into the world shows people whether you have respect for yourself and ultimately whether you deserve theirs. In the words of renowned Canadian psychologist Jordan Peterson:

> If you want to change the world, start by cleaning your room.

I bring to you, Mephibosheth, a man whose presentation was so important it could be argued that it saved his life.

**Meet Mephibosheth**

Few Bible characters provide greater mystery than Mephibosheth. The confusion begins because there are two Mephibosheths if you can believe it! Sort of a biblical Bob. Making it even more challenging to navigate, they both lived in the same time period. If that's not enough, to add yet another thread of complexity to the situation, Mephibosheth and Mephibosheth were related. In fact, Mephibosheth is so confusing as a character that some Bible translators even got it wrong. I opened the chapter with this scripture:

> Mephibosheth, *Saul's grandson*, also went down to meet the king. He had not taken care of his feet or trimmed his mustache or washed his clothes from the day the king left until the day he returned safely.
> —2 Samuel 19:24 NIV

The scripture is quoted from the New International Version. This version is correct; the Mephibosheth being spoken of here was Saul's grandson. However, Mephibosheth is unique in that he confused about half of all Bible translations. For example, the King James Version reads:

> And Mephibosheth *the son of Saul* came down to meet the king, and had neither dressed his feet, nor trimmed his beard, nor washed his clothes, from the day the king departed until the day he came again in peace.
> —2 Samuel 19:24 KJV

One translation refers to Mephibosheth as the grandson of Saul. Another calls Mephibosheth the son of Saul. Of the two, the Mephibosheth discussed *here* is Saul's grandson. One notable distinction between the two was Mephibosheth, the grandson, had been crippled from a young age.

In defense of the King James Version, in biblical reference, the words *son of* can jump generations. For example, the New Testament in Matthew opens by calling Jesus the son of David. Yes, through genealogy, He was a son of David. With this argument, translations that call Mephibosheth the son of Saul are not wrong, per se. However, *in this case* identifying specifically which Mephibosheth is incredibly relevant mainly because one will eventually die a horrible death, while the other is spared.

Now that we've settled all that, let me introduce you to Mephibosheth, son of Jonathan, the *grandson* of Saul. A man so shrouded in mystery, he not only blurred some Bible translations but also seemed to have confused King David. Was he a genius con man with his eye on the throne, or simply protecting his own neck in the kingdom's divide? There are clues arguing both sides. One thing is clear: he knew how to present himself to favor his cause.

After the death of Saul, King David rose to power. At the time it was common practice that when one king won out over another, the rival's family was exterminated to avoid an uprising. Because of this and the numerous attempts at David's life, what few relatives remained in the house of Saul went into hiding.

King David was different. After Saul's death and after the kingdom had settled, he demanded to know if there were any living relatives remaining. He sought not their heads but to show them kindness. For while Saul had been his greatest adversary, Saul's son Jonathan had been David's dearest friend and most loyal companion.

> David asked, "Is there anyone still left of the house of Saul to whom I can show kindness for Jonathan's sake?"
> —2 Samuel 9:1

Ziba, Mephibosheth's servant, was taken before the king to speak of Mephibosheth. He explained that while Mephibosheth was from the family of Saul, he was crippled and could be of little use. Untroubled, King David sent for Mephibosheth immediately. He restored Mephibosheth's land and, without reluctance, opened his arms to his deceased friend's son.

Soon after, the game of thrones continued. King David's own son, Absalom, began to solicit control from the king. In the height of Absalom's rebellion, King David was forced to flee Jerusalem. This left Absalom in the position of power. The people of the kingdom were divided and obligated to choose sides. Some remained within the kingdom in support of Absalom while loyalists followed the king to exile. Mephibosheth remained behind.

Mephibosheth's lead servant, Ziba, went after the fleeing King David. In a show of loyalty, he provided supplies and rumors from within the kingdom. King David inquired as to the whereabouts of Mephibosheth. Ziba shared that Mephibosheth had become a traitor. He claimed that as the grandson of Saul, Mephibosheth was plotting to take control while the father and son argued. On hearing the news, David revoked the land he'd given Mephibosheth and allotted it to his servant, Ziba.

In all the time that King David had been gone, until his return, Mephibosheth had not bathed, trimmed his beard, or even washed his clothes. He certainly hadn't carried himself as a man grooming for the kingship. We are left to only speculate on his motivations, though feigning insanity seems a likely explanation.

Mephibosheth was a citizen of prominence and high standing. In the divide, Absalom had likely paid him a visit to inquire about his loyalties. At this time his servants were left to explain, "Sir, he's gone crazy. Smell him for yourself." It would not have boded well for Mephibosheth if word circulated that he mourned for David. If Absalom were aware that Mephibosheth supported David, upon Absalom's takeover, he surely would have had Mephibosheth executed.

The power struggle and conflict between father and son continued until Absalom came upon a group of David's men in the forest. It was said the terrain was so rough that the land claimed more men than the battles. Absalom became trapped within the thick trees. Surrounded by the king's men, against the king's command, Absalom was killed.

After Absalom's death, King David returned to his place in the kingdom. One of the first to greet him was Mephibosheth. Knowing the king had stripped him of his assets and unsure how King David would react to him, he approached the king humbly.

King David had one simple question for him. "When sides were to be taken, why didn't you follow me?" Mephibosheth replied:

> My lord the king, since I your servant am lame, I said, "I will have my donkey saddled and will ride on it, so I can go with the king. But Ziba my servant betrayed me. And he has slandered your servant to my lord the king."
> —2 Samuel 19:26

Who was to be believed? Ziba or Mephibosheth? Even King David wasn't sure. If he had fully believed one, swift action would have been taken against the other. David was unable to determine the truth. Typical of his rulings, he erred on the side of caution, and he ruled fairly. The land in dispute between Mephibosheth and Ziba was divided equally to both.

After David defeated the revolt from his son, the kingdom regained some semblance of normalcy. However, it was short lived. The Israelites were called to account for a broken oath, and a devastating three-year famine came over the land.

Before King Saul's reign (about four hundred years earlier), Joshua had made an oath to a group of people called the Gibeonites. While it was a peace treaty between the Israelites and the Gibeonites, it was an oath. All Israelites for generations, whether kings or paupers, were to abide by this oath.

When King Saul was in power, he knowingly broke this oath. Not only was Saul responsible for the killing of Gibeonites, but also, on his order, it was done in gruesome and torturous ways.

An oath is not to be confused with a contract. A contract is an agreement meant to be honored. However, sometimes contracts are broken. They can be released or amended. An oath is different. An oath is a solemn promise. Not everyone in life makes a pledge so strong as an oath. It's worth mentioning that presidents do. They are bound by the Oath of Office to preserve, protect, and defend the Constitution of the United States—"so help me God."

> During the reign of David, there was a famine for three successive years; so David sought the face of the Lord. The Lord said, "It is on account of Saul and his blood-stained house; it is because he put the Gibeonites to death."
> —2 Samuel 21:1

David set out to make it right with the Gibeonites. At the time, the Gibeonites were living among the Israelites. This was also part of their agreement from long ago. David called their leaders to his court, and he asked how he could make it right. Their response was brutal, human truth.

They didn't want gold. They didn't want silver. They didn't even ask for food or water in the throes of great famine. They wanted revenge. Their request:

> Let seven of his male descendants be given to us to be killed and their bodies exposed …
> —2 Samuel 21:6

To right the wrong, David agreed. They gathered to attention all the male descendants of Saul. Of the men who stood before him, seven were to be chosen and delivered to the Gibeonites.

What a position to be saddled with, especially for a king like David who had not made his name through unprovoked carnage. Compared to the kings of his time, he was not a confrontational man. Still, seven were to die. Seven were to die *horrible* deaths. By now, stories had already circulated among the Gibeonites of the egregious acts to which Saul had subjected their relatives. You would imagine that they wanted to do the same—or worse—to the unfortunate seven.

Among the relatives of Saul was our Mephibosheth, the grandson of Saul. Now enter the *other* Mephibosheth, the son of Saul and Rizpah, and stepson of Abner.

One was surrendered to the Gibeonites. One was spared.

Our Mephibosheth stood awaiting his judgment. He was one of the only men with whom King David had a known history. Unfortunately for him, the history they had didn't help his cause. Worse yet, it was a strike against him. He'd been accused of being a traitor and plotting a mutiny in the king's absence.

Mephibosheth used his physical appearance to convey a message to those around him. How it was perceived is left to the beholder. Was it a sign of respect, mourning, or sheer insanity? Perhaps it only served to gain him enough sympathy to remain in the king's good graces. Or maybe he was just lucky that David had loved his father, Jonathan.

Mephibosheth's ability to convey a message with only his presence cannot be denied. He had skirted execution during Absalom's revolt. Later he also managed to avoid being handed over in the descendant death lottery. It was the masterful showmanship of Mephibosheth that ultimately led to his life being spared—if not once, but twice.

**Enter Trump**

Trump is an intriguing man. There are many supporters who feel he is the saving grace America needed. There are also those convinced he is rotten to the core. I believe the numbers for the latter group grows smaller with each passing day. Regardless of judgment, there is the undeniable truth: Love him or hate him, he gets people talking. His presentation gets results. Though it may take some time, those results are often his desired results.

February 15, 2016—Greenville, South Carolina. The campaign schedule was at its most grueling. One year in and only nine months until election day, it was the midway point. We were gearing up for spring and the campaign's final push, but winter wasn't through with us yet.

I finished the last rally stop of the day and was headed back to my hotel for the night. The weather was ugly with temperatures in the midtwenties. It was dark and raining. The roads were covered in ice. What little traffic there was on the highway mainly consisted of emergency vehicles. On a patch of black ice on I-385, my car spun a 360. I skidded off the road and came to a slamming stop in a ditch. Thankfully, the eighteen-wheeler behind me left enough distance between us. While he was unable to stop, he honked on repeat as if to say, "Wow! No damage!" My heart was racing, and I immediately realized how very lucky I was.

After shaking off the shock, I drove out and continued to my hotel. Immediately upon check-in, I downloaded and submitted my files to the higher-ups and apologized for my delay. I explained the earlier events, hoping for lenience and understanding. On this day, not one of them reached out to express relief for my safety. I know we were busy, but I confess, it made it hard not to feel small.

March 14, 2015—Hickory, North Carolina. Just a few weeks later, with the crash test still fresh in my mind, I was out on the trail again. That morning, at four o'clock, I hit the road to Hickory. I faced yet another rough ride at the hand of mother nature. That morning, the fog was unbearably thick. Visibility was awful, making the drive painstaking. On arrival I walked through my normal routine. I scouted the surroundings and ensured the area was set for VIP meet and greets. Once complete, I returned to the holding room where the VIPs restlessly awaited Trump's flight arrival. We waited … and waited.

I had a lot to contemplate. At this point I had been chasing the Trump train for more than a year. On that morning, with another risky drive fresh under my belt, I started to question myself. Was all of this running worth it? I was feeling underappreciated, insignificant. I had provided the campaign with the most epic marquee images, requiring no thanks. I had bit my tongue, took orders, bent over backward—all with a smile. I'd submitted every shred of personal information a man possesses. I had stomached grumpy coordinators and added thousands of miles on my car's odometer. I spent time away from my family and my business. I had risked my life. *I had risked my life.*

That day, my friend Pastor Mark Burns was also there to speak and offer a prayer for Mr. Trump. He could see that something wasn't right with me. He asked, and I didn't confess. I was feeling the pressure.

The fog that day was unmanageable. Trump's plane was unable to fly on schedule. Trump Force One tried to make the landing but was forced to wait through the fog. Meanwhile, the event was packed. The crowd was so massive that people were turned away. The VIPs who waited for hours were told that, unfortunately, it wouldn't happen. There simply wasn't time for their one-on-ones with Trump once he was cleared to land.

If I felt I had been run ragged, clutching the end of my rope, I can only imagine what Trump must have felt. Trump kept time very well as a matter of respect, if nothing else. He had always been punctual. One late event, particularly early in the day, meant all other events would be late in the chain reaction.

If I, a minor cog, was disheveled, I couldn't imagine what the wheel must have felt. Up to this point I had never attended an event where he was late, the exception being minor minutes here and there for traffic. But this day we were close to two hours behind the projected start time.

I waited backstage, holding my private pity party for one. To add to the day's frustrations, I had to deal with a totally new lead advance set on dictating my every move. She preferred the "imaginary chalk line" approach and chose my quiet corner to stand in.

When Trump finally rushed in through the back door, a scene that I could have never imagined took place. If only I'd had a camera. Well, let me rephrase that … if only I'd used said camera, I would have the most epic photo ever!

Now, let me tell you—I had heard Trump tell joke after joke about his hair. I don't think most people realize that he's hilarious! Self-deprecating. There were times he invited people on stage to pull his hair to prove that it wasn't a toupee. The crowd would be rolling.

Another time he had us laughing until it hurt. He delivered a stand-up-worthy string of one-liners about how he'd contemplated the effects of global warming because he preferred aerosol hairspray to pump action. Then he went on to mimic the *chht, chht, chht* sound of the individual pumps from the squirt bottle. "We're going to be here all day with pump-action hairspray!"

So let me go back to what happened next on this day. It Trumped everything. I watched as the real-life Donald J. Trump charged in, frustrated and disheveled. He was late, and he did not like to be late. His longtime assistant, Hope Hicks, worked him through the specifics of the event. As she did, she held up a hand mirror, and I watched as Donald Trump fine-tuned his hair—with an aerosol hairspray can. It was like a scene from a movie: backlit, slow motion, and the haze of the hairspray cloud outlined by the sunlight. This moment was everything.

I wanted to take a picture. I *needed* to take a picture. But I didn't dare. This moment will last forever as one of my personal favorite (mental) pictures from the campaign.

Shortly after putting himself together, he stood calmly as though he'd been waiting for hours. He listened for the announcement that called him to the stage.

I was so grateful to have seen him in a moment like that. It proved to me that even the master presenter had his moments. He dusted himself off, threw back his shoulders, and charged in to face the waiting world.

When the event was finished, Trump waved to the crowd and returned backstage. I stood in the corner. I had been there that day to take VIP photos, which we'd had to cancel. I was completely useless. More than anything, my attitude needed a serious adjustment, and the mushroom cloud of hairspray was just the inspiration I needed to get the ball rolling in the right direction. A simple reminder: we're all just doing our best out here.

Trump casually walked off the stage. Then, just out of view from the cheering crowd, he bolted and charged. "Go!" At that, everyone sprang into action to rush him off to his next engagement. As staff hurried about, Trump glanced over at me where I stood, out of the way, in my imaginary chalk-drawn box.

I stood a little taller and waved, my camera still in my palm. On the quiet drive home, I reflected and realized that my attitude was all I had to offer. Anyone with a camera can take pictures. But I was still standing. Mr. Trump appreciated my presentation and showmanship as much as I had realized his.

••••••••••••••••••••••••••••••••••••••••••••••••••••••••••••

One of the greatest honors on the campaign trail was to be a trusted fly on the wall.
Trump would routinely sit down with different perspectives to see where improvements could be made.

On this day, I was given entry before anyone else arrived.
I did what (I think) anyone would do.
I found Trump's seat via his name tag,
and I sat down... just to see what it was like.

I would also, on occassion, take to his podium before Trump took the stage.
I stood where Trump stood, just to take in the view.

The crowd would roar a thunderous "Trump! Trump! Trump!"
It was a thrill.

I wonder what they would have thought backstage if
I had found a way
to get the crowd to shout out
*my* last name on repeat...

Trump became a Trumpet for the Nation.

We are a beautiful & unique group; We are alive and we are waking...
WE are capable of changing the world.

Trump reminded us of our strength and inspired our core.

FOR GOD AND FOR COUNTRY.

# Chapter 8

## Ruth—Ardent Companion

Why have I found such favor in your eyes that you notice me
—a foreigner?
Boaz replied, "I've been told all about what you have done for your mother-in-law since the death of your husband—how you left your father and mother and your homeland and came to live with a people you did not know before."
—Ruth 2:10–11

My wife, Nadean, is a photographer. She had been shooting for years before we married and created quite a following as a wedding photographer. When we did get married, she chose to keep her maiden name professionally. She delivers a classic knee-slapper occasionally when she tells people, "I kept my maiden name for work, but legally I'm a Ho." *Bah-dum-tsst.*

Years ago, she shared a story with me as we decompressed after a workday. She had been shooting a wedding. In attendance were some young guys who happened to be Chinese American. They hadn't been particularly friendly. They hadn't been nasty or inappropriate, simply indifferent to her.

It was then the bride called to them, "Guys, meet my photographer, Nadean. Guess what her last name is?"

In between sips of free booze, they shrugged. That's when the bride told them her last name was Ho. This happened to be the same last name as one of these young men. Their eyes lit up, and they were instantly drawn to Nadean. Later in the evening (after more free bubbly), they even asked to take a selfie with her.

The immersion of the Chinese in America has been unique. Often the Chinese who have immigrated to America readily adopted many of the customs here. In general, we are a rather accommodating crowd, eager and willing to acclimate to American ways. To demonstrate that, my father, who was born in China, was named Ping Kin. Many years ago, when he moved to the states and took his proud place on American soil, he elected to go by Peter.

There are different quirks within any culture, but one commonality is the excitement felt when an outsider can appreciate it. I don't need to guess how these two young men must have felt. Though my wife is not Chinese, they were drawn to her. They could appreciate how much she must love our culture, enough to take it for herself. My wife chose me and the quirks that came with me. In fact, she'd tell you she loves Chinese people so much that she made two of them herself.

To share a little about my family, I have four children, two of them built-in "bonuses" when I met my wife. I've been a part of their lives since they were very young. A few years ago, we had one of those "out of the mouths of babes" moments. These are the kind of memories that are retold through belly laughs at Christmas for decades. While comical, this one was also a lesson in cultural immersion.

At the time, my oldest son, Barry, was in the third grade. The class had been studying different cultures in school, one of them being Chinese. On the drive home, my wife and children discussed what they'd learned. Nadean, amused with where this was going, asked him and my stepdaughter, Ella, if they knew anyone who was Chinese. Both replied with a confident no.

These children had spent years with me. There was the physically obvious proof of me being Chinese. What's more, we lived on blue crabs, pepper steak and rice, and bok choy, and we made our own wontons. We celebrate with tiny red envelopes of lucky money at New Year's (which is *not* on January 1), and we make *juk* in the slow cooker. After five years growing up with me, their innocence never knew to see a difference.

If you can believe it, lightning struck twice. Just a few months ago, my second-grade son, Kruz, was reading a book about the American gold rush. He'd come across a section that detailed accounts of how the Chinese had been persecuted. As he shared, my wife looked at me with a pursed grin (and I knew where she was going). She slowly traced back to him before she asked, "Huh, so do *you* know any Chinese people?" My son, my own Chinese son, said, "Mmm, don't think so!"

In many ways, it was encouraging for us as a society. It had never been something that needed to be a talking point before that moment. He hadn't been mocked, ridiculed, or teased for his last name. Nor had he ever encountered anyone who pointed out his physical aspects.

For me, it was an obvious testament that racism is learned. My own children didn't know I was Chinese. Heck, my own son didn't realize *he* was Chinese. Nor did it matter to them because we had never guided them to believe it was a factor in the world, and hate hasn't found them. The Chinese culture was as normal to them as the big, round earth.

For any culture, there is a great appreciation when someone unfamiliar with it can not only accept but also adopt slivers of it for themselves.

A token reminiscent of this ideal could be found on the campaign trail. Many will likely remember one of the most iconic pieces of swag on the trail: Mr. Trump's classic red hat. Whether it was genius marketing or simply the man's version of dry shampoo, for many it was endearing. It humanized him. The fact of the matter is Trump won Middle America. Some of that could be attributed to simply adopting the good ol' boy's comfort and way of life with the baseball cap.

One might believe the big-city boy would have the lockdown on big-city states. But as history would show, Trump won the heartland. It's a testament to his diversity. It's also a shout to his ability to immerse himself in sentiments of a different way of life. His perceived high-rise lifestyle could have made him a foreigner to the Midwest, but under that baseball cap, he was down-home rural America.

One repeat experience I noticed was that everyone who had met Trump *before* the campaign had a story to share. The stories and their condensed versions all rang to the same tune: Donald Trump is—actually—a really good guy!

No one will ever forget the first time he or she met Donald Trump. For me, as a father … I have one better. I remember the first time Mr. Trump met my wife, Nadean, and son Kruz.

Long before the campaign was officially a campaign, I had the authority to call meet and greets. The chain of command at that time had only enough people to count on one hand. For that, it wasn't exactly moving mountains. I considered people who were influential within their community and asked to arrange meetings when possible.

The irony is it hadn't dawned on me to have Trump meet the most influential person in *my* life: my wife. In part, it was my own shortsightedness. Being in the moment, running from one stop to the next, didn't leave much room for adventure. I admit, another part of me thought it was always going to be there. Then I blinked. Little by little, but seemingly overnight, the campaign went from the tiny hallway of middle school children to massive rallies of tens of thousands.

By the time I had thought to arrange for my wife to meet Trump, the campaign was in its full-blown fervor. My wife and son were set in the VIP area beside the stage where Trump was about to speak.

Meanwhile I was backstage doing the routine prespeech VIP photos. It just so happens that on this day I was also about to live out one of my most memorable mistakes. I know, I know … it's a lengthy list.

Halfway through the VIP line, I did something I had taught for years never to do. For twenty years, I was the photography instructor at Horry-Georgetown Technical College. One of the staples I told my students never to do was touch your subject. And *if* you needed to, you asked permission. Everyone has personal space, his or her "bubble." On the most basic human level, to invade that space can make people uncomfortable. The skill of a talented photographer is being able to instruct your subject how to move by communicating verbally what you need, or by demonstrating it with your actions. But for the love of all things good, never, *ever* physically touch your subject.

With the future president of the United States standing in front of me, I was poised to perfectly apply the lesson I had taught for years. I failed my own instruction. While doing the VIP photos, halfway through, I noticed that Mr. Trump's tie had gone crooked. I swung my cameras over my shoulder, quickly approached Mr. Trump, and squared up his tie.

Admittedly, I have broken my own rules over the years. I had done the same thing a hundred times to rowdy groomsmen. Only this was not a random party bro in a rented suit. This was one of a handful of humans on the planet running for the position of president of the United States of America.

Immediately Trump's main bodyguard, Keith, approached me. He kindly but firmly expressed that under no uncertain terms *ever* repeat that action. There are many reasons why. Some of them I taught. But this time, besides invading a personal bubble, I was holding the neck of our future president in that tie.

After the VIP line and after I groveled an apology to both Mr. Trump and Keith, I went back to the front. After the rally speech, I stood with my wife, and we waited as Trump made his way through the postrally VIP area.

"Mr. Trump!" I said as I directed the attention to my family, "My wife, Nadean, and my son!" My face surely glowed with an expression he hadn't seen from me.

There are things in life you will never forget. *This* was one of mine. I had just gotten chastised for ringing his neck. I feared I was probably about to be fired (again). But in this moment, all those negatives faded. My people, a slice of my everything, were meeting the man I'd spent the better part of a year chasing. With a huge smile and a few nods of father-to-father approval, he simply boasted, "Beautiful. Just beautiful."

He looked at my son so adoringly. My son, a handsome biracial boy, was still so little that he clung to my wife's neck to be high enough to see over the barrier divide. Then Mr. Trump turned to my wife. Genuinely, he thanked her. He confessed how appreciative he'd been for my skill and shared what a wonderful asset I had been. As they closed the conversation, Trump threw his arm around her and stood for a photo with my VIPs.

I'd had my wrists slapped an hour ago for putting Trump in a choke hold. But moments later, as he met my wife and son, it was as if we were at a sunny, casual picnic, sipping sweet tea and rehashing the year's success.

Mr. Trump won me again that day. In his kindness for my family, he made me feel as though he regretted the harsh formalities and the breakneck pace of the campaign, and he treated me as family.

Family isn't always blood.
It's the people in your life who want you in theirs.
—Author unknown

There are few stories that display the beauty of a lasting bond better than Ruth's. Through her devotion to family and appreciation for the people of a foreign land, she carved out her own place in history.

**Meet Ruth**

The story of Ruth is a beautiful one. It is the story of unwavering love despite immense suffering. It is a story demonstrating love for another culture and being adopted by its people. Ruth was a woman willing to set herself aside and fearfully trust the path God had laid for her. This is the story of Ruth:

Thirteen hundred BC—The east was in the throes of another great famine. With food scarce and the land withering, Naomi, her husband, and two sons left their home in Israel. They relocated to the flourishing land of Moab.

While they lived in Moab, Naomi's two sons married local Moabite women. Shortly after the happy occasions, Naomi's husband passed away. Following this, tragically, not one but both of Naomi's sons perished as well. She was left writhing in grief, with her widowed daughters-in-law.

Completely lost in depression, Naomi decided to move back to her home in Israel. She sat with her daughters-in-law to share the news of her decision. She wished to release them from her misery. She insisted they had no responsibility to her and suggested they stay in Moab with their people. She implored them to remarry and build new lives. With this, her daughter-in-law Oprah returned to her parents. Ruth refused. She clung to her mother-in-law:

> But Ruth replied, "Don't urge me to leave you or turn back from
> you. Where you go I will go, and where you stay I will stay.
> Your people will be my people and your God my God.
> Where you die I will die, and there I will be buried.
> May the Lord deal with me, be it ever so severely,
> if anything but death separates you and me."
> —Ruth 1:16–17

Ruth was not a Jew. She was a Moab woman. She was from an area to the east of the Dead Sea, part of a kingdom that was at odds with Naomi's homeland. For your reference, Israel is about the size of New Jersey in square miles, while Moab was smaller than the state of Pennsylvania. In these tight quarters, Israel and Moab (now Jordan) coexisted under different beliefs and separate rule. As a result, many of these kingdoms were often at war with one another. As to be expected with constant turmoil, each of these cultures viewed its system as superior to those around them.

Ruth's decision to stay at Naomi's side in the return to Israel was not only brave but also dangerous. She would face racism and hatred being a Moabite in the kingdom of Judah. But her love for Naomi was greater than her fear of the repercussions.

It was Ruth's deep respect for the culture and the roots of her mother-in-law that earned her reputation and afforded her grace. Ruth lived by the rules of those around her. As a poor Moab woman, she was expected to abide by certain guidelines. When she worked in the fields, she was not allowed to gather crops from the bountiful parts of the field. However, through the culture's version of public assistance, she was allowed to gather scraps from the fields' edges. She worked diligently, respectfully, and without complaint to help provide for her aged mother-in-law.

Perhaps this might explain why Naomi had requested her daughters-in-law not to follow her to Israel. Without their Jewish husbands, Naomi likely predicted the hardships that would befall them in a foreign land.

Eventually Ruth's loyal heart and modest spirit caught the attention of a wealthy landowner named Boaz. Boaz was enamored with Ruth. He recognized her ability to adopt the people and the culture of their land as her own. He saw in her heart a woman capable of putting everything aside for those whom she loved, and they married.

I've been told all about what you have done for your mother-in-law
since the death of your husband, how you left your father and mother and
your homeland and came to live with a people you did not know before.
—Ruth 2:11

Ruth would go on to have an even greater place in biblical history as an ancestral side note. Ruth and Boaz had a son. This son was to be the great-grandfather of King David. From the line of King David, we were brought Jesus Christ.

To those who had believed God's love was only for the Israelites, Ruth's life made a striking contradiction. Proof, yet again, that God sees the heart and chooses whom he will.

Ultimately, it was Ruth's eager willingness to adopt Israel's ways that led to her favorable welcome. Her story shows the value of humility and hard work. Diligently displaying these qualities, she won the hearts of those from whom she sought acceptance.

**Enter Trump**

No one can dispute Mr. Trump's energy level. At this point in the campaign, at age sixty-nine, the man was putting in sixteen- to twenty-hour days. These were the documented hours we could account for. Somehow he still managed to run circles around most of us. Much more was still being done behind the scenes and off the clock. Still, near the end of an incredibly lively day, Trump remained sharp and witty.

I had long buried the events of earlier that day, including the tie debacle. My wife and son had gone home. The campaign charged on, and we changed venues. However, during the last VIP photo line, Trump assured me that he had not forgotten.

Before we started the last group of photos for the day, Trump looked at me with a snicker. He wiggled his tie and joked, "My tie is straight, right?" It was a wonderful gesture to me, delivered in his classic sarcasm. He knew I was concerned and watching out for him. In this simple statement, he offered his willingness to play by the new set of rules I had been given.

Like Ruth, he was always willing to immerse himself into a group and find his way to abide by the rules. I didn't say he wouldn't push the limits of those rules, but he always kept within the lines! Furthermore, if you reread you will notice I said he found *his way* to abide by the rules. In the words of Corey Lewandowski, we let Trump be Trump.

****

Now, to give a quick peek into what kinds of trouble we bumped into, let me further explain. There were two types of floor plans at Trump events. Each option was generally determined simply by the venue space in which we were working. There were events where seating was provided. Then there were events that were primarily standing only.

In some cases, it was theater seating. The upper levels of the arena had seats, as well as the floor. This meant directly in front of the stage there were *actual* seats. One seat, one person.

These events were so much easier to navigate. With space to move in, it was significantly easier for me to photograph as well.

The other possible arrangement was more of a free-for-all. What this meant was the floor level was shoulder-to-shoulder. This layout was incredibly difficult to navigate. Even if you toted an official staff pass, it was slow getting through the sea of disorganized supporters.

No matter the seating situation, it was the responsibility of the local fire marshal to determine when to close out attendance. Trump rallies were free events. Without a read on ticket sales, gauging the crowd size was done live. At issue was the cut-off capacity, which was at the mercy and judgment of the fire marshal.

Here is where the problem came in. Our fire marshal on this day was lowering the boom. He prepared to shut the door, closing attendance.

Now I don't believe Trump is guilty of questioning authority. No, Mr. Trump, by nature, is a man who questions *everything*. For that, he can stumble into options that would have otherwise never been on the table. As they say, you can't have what you don't ask for.

In action he worked to reach middle ground when problems did rise. He was well versed in utilizing his abilities to hold a conversation aimed at reaching an agreement. On the campaign trail, we encountered all kinds. It's a true testament to his ability to "chameleon" his way into a community and find a way to be accepted within it.

On this day, the arena had filled up quickly. There were still hundreds in line outside waiting to get in. (Though this wasn't an uncommon occurrence, the media seldom reported it.) Trump arrived backstage, and we immediately went into VIP pictures. Just as we finished, one of the staffers approached solemnly. It appeared to be unfavorable news.

I'm an illustrious fly on the wall. That might sound like an oxymoron, to be proudly known for being forgotten, but to be seen and not heard was one of my greatest assets in the candid journalism forum. Normally, when conversations were had with Trump while I was an arm's length away, I did my best not to hear. On this occasion, however, there was some setback news. And it was being delivered by a lead advance who hadn't been especially kind to me. Full disclosure: I hung around for the show.

"Sir, the fire marshal is going to shut down attendance."

"What's it looking like out there?" Trump asked.

He detailed an accurate report of about how many people were still outside paired with the floor's estimated stats.

"Ask the fire marshal to come back here to speak with me," Trump said.

About ten minutes later, the lead advance returned with more bad news.

"Mr. Trump," he stammered, "he refused to come back here."

When it came to Trump-mania, you expected everyone said yes, right?

Well, this fire marshal outright said no. Twice. I don't have a firsthand account of just what was said or how he managed it. What I do know is moments later there was a closed-door conversation between the fire marshal and Trump. On the fire marshal's terms and on his turf, Mr. Trump walked out having gotten his way.

Once the event started, the line from outside had made its way into the room. On taking the podium, the first thing Mr. Trump did was thank the fire marshal for his gracious hospitality in their great city. He mentioned the beautiful local following and implored the media to turn their cameras to show the enthusiastic room, brimming at full capacity.

Respect, understanding, and a noted willingness to abide by house rules was his method of operation. I'd seen this negotiation play out other times. He is truly a man of middle ground. His eyes see vibrant options for resolve when others see black and white.

Later in the campaign I remember a round table sit-down. It wasn't a hush-hush, top-secret event. At this event a few high-tier businessmen were granted a moment at our candidate's ear.

I readily recognized many of the people at the table. It was a who's who in business. Ironically, I didn't recognize the man Mr. Trump sat next to. As Trump settled into his chair, he promptly inquired of this man's field. (Pause: Donald Trump, the man with a golden signature, would like to know what *you* do for a living. Just imagine the pressure.)

With slight hesitation, the man explained that he was the owner of fast-food franchises. He quickly rattled off three or four well-known franchises.

"Fast food? Of all your franchises, which one does the best for you?" Trump asked, leaning in.

The man's eyes lit up. He shared how differing franchises required different strategy. He detailed the pros and cons, and told which were strong and why. He went on to discuss how seasonal influences impacted each differently. Meanwhile Trump listened, engrossed. Businessman to businessman (with wallflower businessman listening to tell you …), it was a genuinely awesome exchange.

Trump opened the door into this man's world. But more importantly, he cared to listen once that door was open.

For Trump, as one American to another, the truth always found its way:

And your people will be my people.

The general media had to stay in a designated area we called "The Pit."
Meanwhile, I had the liberty to roam the room for alternate angles...
if I could make my way through the enthusiastic crowd.

# Chapter 9

## Ahithophel—The Unbridled Counselor

Ahithophel told him, "Go and sleep with your father's concubines,
for he has left them here to look after the palace.
Then all Israel will know that you have insulted your father
beyond hope of reconciliation, and they will throw their support to you."
—2 Samuel 16:21

According to the Merriam-Webster dictionary, the definition of *wisdom* is the ability to think and act, using *knowledge*, *experience*, *understanding*, *common sense*, and *insight*. It doesn't appear to be a dealer's choice of *most* of these qualities. The definition requires all of them, in unity. Each one of these qualities, while valuable on their own, is weaker without the mastery of the others. Wisdom is a massively complex, lifelong undertaking.

The physical makeup of the human brain tells us the ingredients are processed in completely different departments. The right side of our brain harbors the emotions, intuition, and creativity, while the left side argues for logic, reasoning, and analysis. The construct of a mortal makes it a feat of argument within our own heads.

Emotion versus logic:
What we feel doesn't always agree with what we know.

Wisdom requires intellectual honesty and great dedication to achieve. It takes years of self-study, humility, and reflection to admit personal weakness exists. And it takes additional years still to face those shortcomings honestly, with the desire to change them.

Biblically speaking, the fear of the Lord is the beginning of wisdom:

The fear of the Lord is the beginning of wisdom,
and knowledge of the Holy One is understanding.
—Proverbs 9:10

To achieve wisdom through fear made little sense until I became a father. This verse is easier understood said in reverse: Wisdom *begins* with the fear of the Lord. If there is a beginning, then this is a process … a journey to the desired end, which, I believe, is no longer to fear God but to respect him as your Heavenly Father and to see more clearly His wishes for you, His child.

Fear > Obedience > Understanding > Respect > Wisdom

Just like the relationship with your earthly father, what begins in youth as a fear of scolding evolves into an understanding of what is right and becomes a desire to make him proud. As you lace the shoes of your own son, you realize that your father was the fearful one—fearful for you. He was afraid that you would get lost or that you would be hurt. He prayed you would find the right friends and a suitable spouse, and you would live with great purpose.

God does not want us to live *in fear*. He wants us to grow to become respectful adults, so versed in understanding the repercussions of doing wrong that we've learned to live wisely. That is the hope of a great father: that his children learn to live well.

My father-in-law was one such man. He was humble, patient, and God-fearing. He was truly one of the wisest men I have ever met. He inspired others around him to do better. He led quietly and simply by living well.

That was Gerald Bruehlman. He was born and raised in a small farming village in southern Wisconsin. He delighted in being needed, and he loved his place in life. He was satisfied. He worked for the village. There he rebuilt streets and maintained water quality. For thirty years, he was a volunteer fireman and an EMT. On the occasion the congregation's pastor was away, Gerald would step in to write and give the sermon for church on Sunday.

There was no end to the tasks he would take on, without a second thought. I had asked him once why on earth he had taken the coroner's position. He shrugged and said, "Eh, somebody's gotta do it—and I can."

He was never one to use his wisdom to acquire great riches. That wasn't his motivation in life. I once heard him say if he had the winning lottery ticket in his hand, he'd tear it up. He swore it would ruin your life. Every thread of me knows, he meant it. He lived well by seeking God's will.

Gerald was diagnosed with stage 4 glioblastoma multiforme at the age of forty-eight. Surgery was performed to remove the baseball-sized tumor. Unfortunately, it had crushed a portion of the communication center in his brain. This rendered him unable to read, and he had great difficulty recalling speech. Through his final years, he sat with his Bible and a legal pad as he retraced the words his heart knew.

On February 23, 2015, Gerald passed away from brain cancer. The town stopped bustling. They lined the streets with flags, fire trucks, squad cars, and servicemen. For hours people filtered through to pay their respects. "Don't regret growing older," he had said. "It's a privilege denied to many."

One of the most touching ways that my father-in-law applied wisdom was through the words he left with his daughter—my wife, Nadean. What mattered to him most was to know his family was cared for, and they would have continued guidance in life.

On her last visit with him, my wife pledged that she would care for and help lead them. My father-in-law inspired others; he used his faith in us to bring out the best in us.

He responded directly, "Enjoy it." He meant humbly, "Don't do it for me. Don't do it for them. Do it for you. Find pleasure in serving others."

On an old corkboard he kept at work were found snippets into what led him daily. Alongside a few photographs of family was a weathered old poem. He found inspiration in its words. He carried them daily. He lived *and died* with courage and confidence.

Written in the 1950s by Heartsill Wilson, it was a piece entitled "A New Day." It's a powerful poem that cuts to the core of purpose, with ultimate wisdom. Thanks to Gerald, I live by the same words now. Perhaps you, too, will find inspiration in the words he cherished:

**A New Day**

This is the beginning of a new day.
God has given me this day to use as I will.
I can waste it—or use it for good.
What I do today is very important
Because I am exchanging a day of my life for it!
When tomorrow comes,
This day will be gone forever,

Leaving in its place something I have traded for it.
I want it to be gain, and not loss;
Good and not evil;
Success and not failure;
In order that I shall not regret the price I have paid for it.

This is my day of opportunity and duty.
Today I will live with courage and confidence.

**Meet Ahithophel**

The task to offer only one biblical character the title of wisdom was no easy feat. There are so many great men and women who displayed wisdom. Many did so in unique and challenging circumstances. My hope is to offer new concepts for discussion and alternate viewpoints that may not have previously been considered. For that, I present to you a worthy contender in Ahithophel.

Ahithophel was a very wise man, renowned for his advice and guidance. His reputation for amazing counsel was so well known that he was asked to serve as an adviser to King David.

Many of us know someone in our own lives who is similar—the person you can go to with any problem. No matter how profound or complex the issue, he or she has the words to ease you. That person's opinion and counsel is respected so greatly that even when the advice is a little unconventional, you follow it faithfully.

Ahithophel was most known for his strongest attribute. Remember, no *one* thing can fully define us:

Ahithophel was an incredibly wise counsel.
Ahithophel was a traitor.

Ahithophel was in King David's inner circle, a trusted adviser and friend. However, during the fallout between King David and his son, Absalom, Ahithophel went rogue. He betrayed King David and turned his support to the up-and-coming Absalom.

The dynamics for insiders must have been quite confusing to navigate. Ahithophel had been a trusted counsel to the king. While the king and his son had a very public fallout, everyone was forced to declare their allegiance. In the division, Ahithophel stayed within the comforts of the kingdom and gave his support to the perceived winner, Absalom. In addition to his support, Ahithophel also provided his coveted guidance to Absalom, the combatant son.

If, for David, the betrayal wasn't enough, the advice Ahithophel gave to Absalom was shockingly brutal. It was brilliant wisdom used for great detriment. This was guerilla warfare, circa 1025 BC. Ahithophel's advice created a divisive, unethical conspiracy, designed to break the king and throw power to the rising Absalom.

Ahithophel's plan for him was simple. He advised Absalom to make a public display of his power. To do this, he suggested that Absalom sleep with his father's concubines.

This was not merely a lustful dalliance heard through the grapevines and discussed in the king's daily briefing. A tent was raised where it would be clearly visible to the masses. Then, one after another, King David's concubines filtered in and out of Absalom's tent. This was expertly plotted by Ahithophel to ensure everyone in the city knew that Absalom asserted charge now.

Prior to this, many Israelites hadn't chosen sides between the father and son. This act proved reconciliation was now out of the question. Sides were to be taken.

When David discovered that Ahithophel had betrayed him and was advising Absalom, he was distraught.

> Now in those days the advice Ahithophel gave was like that of one who inquires of God. That was how both David and Absalom regarded all of Ahithophel's advice.
> —2 Samuel 16:23

Ahithophel continued to share winning advice and wisdom with the rising power, Absalom. Concerned, David prayed to God and asked Him to confuse Ahithophel's advice. While the Lord had never left David, He did not provide the king with this request. Just because you've made a request of the Lord doesn't erase your responsibility to help yourself in the situation.

King David was not a novice in unrest and war. Upon leaving the kingdom, many of his faithful supporters had come to him, asking how they might help. For their safety, he turned many of them away. However, there were a few that he held as trusted confidants, despite the betrayal of others. With their help, he set a countercoup in motion.

David, in *his* wisdom, took advantage of the offers to help. He created a small, stealth group of insiders. Two young priests and a dear friend named Hushai made up the quiet intel plants. Little by little, the group of loyalists quietly returned to the city that Absalom had overtaken. Upon their return, they humbly threw their support and respect to young Absalom. Quick to receive a compliment, Absalom welcomed them with open arms.

As the unrest continued, war was imminent. Absalom asked for direction on how to destroy King David's army. For guidance on how to proceed, he asked Ahithophel. Ahithophel stood before him. He suggested that Absalom assemble an army of twelve thousand to surge immediately, that night. The desired objective: kill the ill-prepared King David, with no other casualties, and return to the kingdom.

Absalom took the words to heart. However, in the uncertain times, he requested a second opinion and called to attention Hushai. Hushai suggested that this time Ahithophel's advice might not be the proper strategy. He proceeded to build a superior attack, with significantly larger numbers and a plan to annihilate all who were loyal to the king. Absalom agreed; Hushai's strategy sounded the better of the two.

Immediately upon leaving Absalom's quarters, Hushai sent his men to David with detailed information about his conversation.

So, while David had prayed to God that Ahithophel's advice be confused, it wasn't. God still required the individual will of David to create the outcome. Instead of God confusing the wisdom of Ahithophel, Absalom was given a second opinion. Unbeknownst to him, the second opinion he received was from a secret agent in David's camp.

Gossip and chatter had worked both ways. King David had asked the Lord to confuse Ahithophel's advice, which led Absalom and his men to question Ahithophel's wisdom. When the advice of Hushai seemed to far surpass that of Ahithophel's, Absalom chose against Ahithophel to his peril.

In the end, neither Ahithophel nor Absalom survived the fateful course they had set in motion. It may seem a bit ironic that we've detailed the wisdom of Ahithophel here when it wound up being the superior wisdom of David that won.

There's always going to be someone out there who is smarter than you are. Acting like there isn't proves it.

## Enter Trump

For those who closely followed the campaign and beyond, you've witnessed Trump's cunning wisdom in full display. The Trump community has been known to say he is working ten moves ahead of the rest of the players. They argue he's playing 4-D chess. From the inside of the campaign, I concede, it was naive to deny his wisdom. Trump's rise to the political top was due, in part, to his keen ability to play coy. He didn't make a habit of advertising his strategy, and it's clear that was the strategy, in and of itself.

From the beginning Trump used his wealth of *knowledge* in business to take charge. He commanded leadership as the boss. He worked long hours and demonstrated the best way to lead was by example.

You didn't need to be up close and personal to see him dominate the ring. He was the centerpiece of political debates. He ran circles around the others at rallies, and most notably, he owned the media coverage. (He didn't legally own the media because that would be a conflict of interest. America would see through that bias immediately, right?) Trump was clever. He used the media's public displays like Ahithophel used the king's concubines.

> The point is that if you are a little different, or a little outrageous, or if you do things that are bold or controversial, the press is going to write about you.
> —Donald Trump

Trump commanded the press. The reports were generally skewed to show him in the worst light possible, but in *The Art of the Deal*, he writes, "Good publicity is preferable to bad, but from a bottom-line perspective, bad publicity is sometimes better than no publicity at all."

This idea was brought to center stage with the results of a study done in March 2016, conducted by the *New York Times*. The results showed media coverage that was bought, compared to given freely, for each candidate at the time. Free media coverage for the top Democratic candidate at the time was estimated at $746 million. Meanwhile Trump's free media coverage came in at nearly $2 billion.

A more comprehensive study might include how much of the media's echo chamber was used to show him in a positive light.

There were times we drew a deep breath into our lungs when we read the latest, shaking our heads and wondering how he would overcome the headlines. Yet somehow he always did. For all that has come to light since the 2015–16 campaign days, I've looked back in awe that he was able to hold his tongue as well as he did.

He carried his *experience* after navigating the press for years. Mr. Trump is well versed in the inner workings of publicity. He utilized it to obtain a voice decades before his run for the presidency. Using that know-how, there were times we watched Trump play the media like a cheap fiddle. Sometimes we knew it as it unfolded; other times future proved past.

One entertaining instance we got to see in real-time was in September 2016. Trump offered the media a news conference. At the time, the media was terribly interested in revisiting the Obama birth issue. Trump promised a special announcement regarding the topic. He welcomed them to his newly opened Washington, DC, hotel. In a blink Trump had three cable news outlets running him live on their networks. On live television, for nearly thirty minutes, the Trump camp held court.

He took the opportunity to genuinely thank our courageous military heroes for their service to our country. Then he offered the mic to numerous highly decorated veterans and Medal of Honor winners. They proceeded to give their powerfully emotional endorsements for Mr. Trump as president. Donald Trump did, in fact, make good on his promise to the media. In his final thirty seconds on stage, he acknowledged the Obama birth issue and insisted it was time to move on to something with relevance.

The media was virtually fixated on Trump. Like a president calling a press corps for an important announcement, he did so as a candidate, at will. Prior to running for president, Mr. Trump, as a celebrity, had the wherewithal to take advantage of the media's eagerness to cover him. He had the *understanding* to realize that being a contender for commander in chief lent him a much larger platform.

Quite brilliantly, Trump used the media. If they were offering to prostitute their pen, he was ready to take advantage of their willingness. At times, it seemed the press was but a necessary evil in the campaign process. There was a love/hate relationship that we still see playing out in the headlines. You've heard it said: if Trump pardoned the Thanksgiving turkey, the media would report he forced his family to go hungry.

While with Trump, I carried a camera. Luckily, I was not categorized as part of the media. I was his personal campaign photographer. In the beginning of the campaign process, there was little media in attendance. The media and I roamed free. The photojournalists could go anywhere they chose, as could I. The only difference between me and the other photographers was that I had the liberty to go backstage.

Once the campaign went into full swing, and the numbers began to rise, more restrictions and organization were needed. It was at this time, the press was assigned an area in the middle of the arena, dubbed "the pit." The area was literally fenced off. The press was free to roam the venue until about an hour before Trump took the stage. Then those with media passes had to check in to receive access to the pit. At entry, there was one person responsible for overseeing the media inside. Some of the gatekeepers really enjoyed their authority over the press.

There was one media manager in particular who thoroughly enjoyed his role. In addition to bathroom rejections, he would make the press wait thirty minutes *after* the talk before he would allow them to leave the holding pen. This was humiliating I'm sure, yet the mighty press willingly obeyed. To take that a step further, he also required staffers escort the media out after their thirty-minute hold. But there was little to no resistance, other than mumbles under their breath. The absence of argument was easy to understand. If they didn't comply, they could have their press credentials pulled for future Trump events. Not one of them was so naive to ignore the fact that Trump sells.

Months later I asked the particularly strict media manager why he kept the rules he did for the pit. His response was simply, "Eh, why not?"

It was open season on the press. For years no one questioned their boldened letters. No one questioned their motives. Americans faithfully believed their self-proclaimed "trusted news sources." Trump took the first public step in questioning that perhaps, just maybe, the mainstream media was nothing more than a lady of the night under all those fancy lights. Bought and sold.

Trump's campaign was his. He owned it. *Common sense* drove him to ensure it was all his. If not beholden to special interests, he could not be called to disobey his moral compass.

He spent decades in the company of politicians, watching them dance for the money. He made sure there was no confusion about his leadership, asserting dominance immediately. The media understood the value of the content he could provide them. He was in control, in a league all his own, carrying wisdom he learned through the years.

It was early on that I could clearly see Mr. Trump was destined for great things as POTUS. If it was nothing more than his dignity that drove him, his pride was always enough.

Donald Trump knew how to play the game. We've all heard him talk about winning. He likes to win. He has a readiness for it, and Donald Trump is a very patient fighter. The *insight* and discernment he collected over the years had molded him into the man who would allow the media to paint him as a loser in order to win.

****

Man is made or unmade by himself. The pursuit of knowledge, experience, understanding, common sense, and insight map the path to wisdom. Still, having a map doesn't guarantee one will arrive at his or her destination. It takes conscious effort and a focused objective to work relentlessly toward personal improvement. Wisdom is not a set destination but found in the journey. Through that journey, the truth boils down to one human philosophy:

Wisdom comes from living well.

Thursday, November 3rd, 2016 - the week before THE Election Day.
Trump held an event on a farm outside Selma, NC.

The attendance was through the roof, so luckily there wasn't one.

To entertain my interest, I found the rear-most position to take
the obligatory crowd-shot for the night.
Faithfully, his supporters stood
at a distance that binoculars were necessary.

It was a rare outdoor event.
With the Election just days away,
celebratory fireworks concluded Trump's speech.

American Pride was running on all cylinders.

# Chapter 10

## Deborah—A True Leader

Barak said to her, "If you go with me, I will go;
but if you don't go with me, I won't go."
"Certainly I will go with you," said Deborah.
"But because of the course you are taking, the honor will not be yours,
for the Lord will deliver Sisera into the hands of a woman …"
—Judges 4:8–9

Ponder with me the dominant characteristics of successful companies. What makes them succeed? Traits like strong leadership, clever marketing, a focused objective, and great service come to mind. But on that short list, one major factor in building something great is teamwork. A unified group working toward a common goal is practically unstoppable.

In my home, we aren't big television people. We own a television, but it's rarely on. Maybe I should rephrase: *It may be watching us, but we don't watch it.* In this day and age, the talking points carry without hours spent with the TV.

Over the last few generations, game shows have been a popular American pastime. Classic game shows gave way to reality television and then merged to birth the reality competition genre. It's amusing, isn't it? Who could have thought that a game-show host would go on to be (arguably) one of the best presidents in United States history? Donald Trump was already a celebrity and a business icon, but he went from having a niche following to becoming a household staple when he took on the face of *The Apprentice.*

Like *The Apprentice*, one of the long-standing greats in reality competition is *Hell's Kitchen*, which premiered in 2005. It's akin to *The Apprentice* in that contestants compete against one another in a series of challenges, but for *Hell's Kitchen* the objective is culinary genius. While winning is gravy, many of the top finishers go on to find careers from the publicity.

The fourth season runner-up was a chef by the name of Lou Petrozza. By chance encounter after season 4 aired, Petrozza made his way south to my hometown of Myrtle Beach. He took a position as chef at a high-end local restaurant called 21 Main. This restaurant offers a banquet hall, where many weddings and other glitzy affairs take place. Quick to capitalize on Petrozza's fame from the show, the restaurant manager asked me to coordinate promotional pictures of their newly hired celebrity chef.

The restaurant was smart to promote Petrozza as the face of their kitchen. It was clever marketing as customers would say, "Well, you know who the chef is? … He's the guy from *Hell's Kitchen*!"

It wasn't unusual for guests at weddings to hope they might meet him. Inevitably, by the night's end, the newly married couple would coax Chef Lou out of the kitchen. In a classic white chef's coat and flaming-red chili pepper pants, he would happily oblige to pose for selfies. He had a larger-than-life presence, and his never-met-a-stranger personality fed the restaurant's buzz.

The year following Petrozza's hire, I photographed Myrtle Beach's annual Taste of the Town. Held at the convention center, Taste of the Town is an opportunity for businesses to come together in friendly competition and showcase their menu favorites. The premise is competing restaurants prepare their marquee dish for a panel of select judges. The winner earns bragging rights for the year as Myrtle Beach's Best of the Beach.

The event is mostly a social affair for locals to unwind following the tourist season. However, at the end of the night, they announce the winners. While a restaurant hopes to win Best Dessert or Best Appetizer, the crème de la crème is People's Choice—Best Entrée. That year, 21 Main walked away with the coveted title.

The 21 Main team piled in for the obligatory group picture with their trophy. Following the onslaught of backslaps and Italian hugs, the restaurant's general manager, John Mungavin, requested an individual portrait of their executive chef. I began scanning their crew for Chef Lou. Then the executive chef stepped forward. Only it wasn't Chef Lou. The executive chef at 21 Main was Chef Corey Johnson. Chef Lou was *one* of their chefs, but he was not the mastermind behind their culinary win.

It was an incredible display of humility and teamwork on all accounts. Chef Corey was content to lead the kitchen from the back. He happily passed the paparazzi and spotlight to the reality television chef, while he did what he does best. On the other end of things, Chef Lou, who was riding fresh off the fame of *Hell's Kitchen*, sat back and took orders from another chef. Their willful collaboration of talent and teamwork brought success for both chefs and their kitchen.

****

Another account of humility and teamwork hits a little closer to home. My wife, Nadean, has been a photographer for Gene Ho Photography, Inc., for fourteen years. Virtually anyone who has attempted to compete with her knows that Nadean is the driving force—the "master chef"—of the wedding photography industry. I take my technical advice from my wife, and she's a savage perfectionist.

Long before I started with the Trump campaign, I was already well known for a specific technique. I became almost famous in the photographic community for my application of the fish-eye lens. My technique was particularly useful in low-light situations from an ultra-low angle. Companies in the photography world took notice, and I was sponsored to give lectures on the topic. I filmed a YouTube video on the topic that has received nearly half a million views, a notable number considering the US Bureau of Labor reports only fifty-thousand professional photographers in the United States.

In joining the campaign, I used this unique approach with Donald Trump. Until this point, it had not been done. I was the lone photographer with a 10.5 fish-eye in a sea of gargantuan telephoto lenses. To me, it just made sense. The wide-angle fish-eye's strength and purpose is capturing your "where." In a time when the mainstream media was reluctant to report Trump's following, the fish-eye was able to embody the truth.

Well, this masterfully genius technique that I've implemented and made gains from was invented by my wife. She pioneered this style of photography, and I mimicked her.

When I was on the speaking circuit teaching these techniques, I traveled to stages in Las Vegas, Atlanta, and New Orleans. I recall one event in Las Vegas where I was speaking to a group of photographers. The crowd was absolutely roaring with laughter through my presentation. Afterward, one of my staff photographers looked at me and shook her head. "You ripped off Nadean's jokes too?" I was busted. In my defense, she's got excellent comedic material.

Thankfully, she doesn't mind me taking the spotlight. We're on the same team, focused on the same goals. Nadean has let me walk out the door for years to soak up the accolades she deserves. Meanwhile, I don't mind taking the back seat when brides hire my protégé over me. It's easier to lose to your apprentice when the apprentice is your wife.

I'd like to share with you the story of a woman like my wife. Deborah was a leader whose focus on the win was greater than the concern for who would be credited with it.

## Meet Deborah

As the father of two young ladies and the husband of a powerhouse, I know well: women rule the world. It never ceases to amaze me how something so small can be so fiercely intense. I've got sugar and an extra heap of spice with my girls, and I intend to keep the stars on their courses. God's speed, future husbands.

It is crucial in growing strong women that we center them on principles they control. We praise *who they are* and not the package they came in. Beauty does not define them. Empower the women in your life to take their natural God-given gifts, and let them run wild. Women are born leaders. What better way of reminding them of this than pointing them to amazingly brave examples.

I bring to you the story of Deborah, an inspiring woman who knew when to lead and when to trust.

Deborah was a judge in mid-1100 BC. We touched on another judge earlier with Ehud. Deborah's time was a few years later. She was a revolutionary leader and served as a compass, directing the people of Israel back to the word of God.

Deborah was a matter-of-fact military commander. She led by means of unification and teamwork. In winning, it didn't matter who took credit, only that the goal was achieved. Those qualified were asked to the task for God and for country.

With Deborah there were no guarantees of being hailed a hero. She led with a "united we stand" mentality, and a win for one was a win for all. It was this prevailing attitude that she hoped to inspire in her military commander, Barak.

During Deborah's days, the people of Israel had fallen again. They found themselves under the tyrannical reign of the Canaanites. The enemy army was a mighty force with technology that surpassed that of the Israelites. The militia they faced consisted of nine hundred iron chariots and was led by the beastly Sisera. In their desperate pleas for relief, God gave them Deborah.

Deborah set out to coordinate her troops, ten thousand strong. She put them under the command of Barak. She formulated a strategy to create a decoy. She planned to lure the enemy camp to the river. Cornered at the riverside, Barak and the group of ten thousand would lay siege to them.

Upon sharing the well-devised battle plans with comrades, Commander Barak replied with a weak no. Well, he didn't exactly say no. He said he would go if she went with him, but he wasn't going to go unless she did. I'm trying to imagine how this would work in my life:

Wife: "Honey, could you toss that load of dishes in, please?"
Me: "No, I'll only load the dishes in if you do it with me."

As juvenile as it sounds, Barak wouldn't go alone. Ten thousand soldiers were not enough; he demanded that Deborah go with him. She quickly snapped back:

"Certainly I will go with you," said Deborah. "But because of the course you are taking, the honor will not be yours, for the Lord will deliver Sisera into the hands of a woman."
—Judges 4:9

A woman would be given the credit? *Of course, she would.* Barak could bet if Deborah was going to do his job for him, she was going to take the glory in victory. Keeping good on his word, Barak agreed to proceed with Deborah leading the charge.

Deborah would have known with unwavering certainty that they would come out the victors. She was not only a judge, but she was also a prophetess, meaning God communicated with her. While not all prophets were judges, not all judges were prophets. Deborah, a remarkable woman, was both.

As Deborah had predicted, Barak and the Israelite entourage overcame Sisera's army. As the battle ended, one Canaanite remained. When he realized the unexpected defeat, Sisera fled on foot. Barak took pursuit, but Sisera escaped.

Now Sisera wasn't an ordinary military commander. He was an infamous general, particularly noted for his size. You may remember another better-known Canaanite, Goliath (of David and

Goliath). Canaanites were believed to be descendants of the fallen angels, and some were born with extraordinary strength and unfathomable size. Sisera was like Goliath in stature but with an advanced army at his disposal, Sisera seemed all the more unconquerable.

This would explain Barak's original reluctance. It could also shed light on how Sisera, the general and lone survivor of the battle at the river, managed to get away *on foot*. Perhaps Barak's pursuit of the fleeing Canaanite giant wasn't as feverish as it could have been.

Imagine if Barak had the same courage as David, who was to come years later. David, at just fifteen years of age, took on the infamous giant of his time. The Sunday school lessons could have been that of Barak and Sisera, but alas …

After fleeing from battle, Sisera looked for a safe haven. Seeing him flee, Jael, the wife of Heber, called to him and offered her tent as refuge. She hurried him inside and hid him away.

> Sisera, meanwhile, fled on foot to the tent of Jael, the wife of Heber the Kenite, because there was an alliance between Jabin king of Hazor and the family of Heber the Kenite.
> —Judges 4:17

Two things are of noted relevance here. First, Jael welcomed Sisera into her *tent*, not her house. Jael and her husband, Heber, lived in Zaanaim, which means wandering. They chose to live apart from society as nomads. A likely explanation was that in the moral decay of humanity at the time, they chose to isolate themselves from society.

Secondly, the alliance that was made wasn't made with Jael. It was made between Jabin (Sisera's boss) and the *family* of Heber and Jael. Heber and Jael had nothing to do with the politics of things.

Jael took him into her tent.

> "I'm thirsty," he said. "Please give me some water." She opened a skin of milk, gave him a drink, and covered him up.
> —Judges 4:18–19

Exhausted from the battle and weary from the escape, he asked her for water. She cordially returned—with milk. (Maybe water would have been too difficult to conceal a foreign agent?) Grateful for anything, Sisera accepted and drank what was given. She tucked him in after his warm milk. Then he asked that she keep watch for those in pursuit, so he could sleep. Jael obliged.

> But Jael, Heber's wife, picked up a tent peg and a hammer and went quietly to him while he lay fast asleep, exhausted. She drove the peg through his temple into the ground, and he died.
> —Judges 4:21

As they say, if you're going to swing at the giant, you'd better swing hard, and you'd better not miss. Jael had one shot. She hadn't gotten out of bed that morning knowing what it would hold for her, but like a strong woman will, she owned it. She saw an opportunity. With one swift act, she could end the unrest between two camps. While she personally had no allegiance to either side, she took the opportunity to end the conflict.

As Deborah had foretold, the glory belonged to a woman. But it wasn't for herself as Barak might have assumed. It was for Jael, the unforeseen third party. Jael was an ironic nominee for the position, considering she lived as a nomad to avoid conflict. Still, as we've seen in action numerous times already, God chooses whom He will.

Deborah could have easily accepted credit for the win she orchestrated. However, through her songs of victory, Deborah ensured that Jael was heralded the heroine. As the leader of Israel, Deborah led by example with unity, focused on the greater good. As a great mother of Israel, she knew the value of humility and teamwork, and she shared the glory.

**Enter Trump**

It goes without saying that Trump was the centerpiece of the campaign. We all had a role in it to give him support. Without the king on the chessboard, we were a loose group of American pawns with dreams of change. Still, Trump had an obligation, and he knew it. The core of his hopeful position was that he was beholden to a new boss: us.

When someone decides to start a business of his or her own, the usual response from others is "Wow! It'll be so great to be your own boss." Those people have likely never owned a business. Those who have experience in business ownership know that with your product or service, you are now responsible for pleasing paying clients, your new employer. You've successfully exchanged your old (singular) boss for hundreds or thousands of new bosses. All those bosses are controlled by the worst tyrant of them all: *you*.

Trump had a marked appreciation for those whom he now worked for. One group I watched him give special attention to were the men and women who serve our country—at home and abroad. It was a regular feature of the campaign that the VIP line would include a group of selected first responders, police, fire, military, etc. These men and women were called in at his request.

On November 3, 2016, the final days of the campaign were upon us, and one of the final rallies was held. In attendance was an honored group of American heroes, our Medal of Honor recipients. The Medal of Honor is the highest military decoration the United States government presents to a member of its armed forces. It is bestowed upon those who served with valor, at the risk of their life, above and beyond the call of duty. It is a rare and distinguished award. Currently, there are only seventy-one living recipients of this prestigious award. Of the seventy-one, there were eight Medal of Honor recipients in attendance on this day. The small group of courageous war heroes was poised to meet and shake the hand of our Republican candidate, Donald J. Trump.

At this event, in familiar fashion, we started short on time. To make it up, I suggested that we take the Medal of Honor recipients as a group photo. Within earshot, one of the honored veterans looked at us with a steely gaze that demanded our attention. He shook his head to deny my remark and sternly said, "No, sir. Individually." Trump looked back at me as if I had power over time. His tough-as-nails American "boss" had spoken. Trump wasn't going to tell the war hero no, and neither was I.

****

Trump and his crew demonstrated the epitome of teamwork and humility, primarily credited to his original team being his longtime core. Long before White House talks, way back in 1999, Trump hired his bodyguard and director of security, Keith Schiller. Other than Trump's wife and biological family, if I had to guess whom he most trusted, I would have said Keith Schiller. He had been at Trump's side for nearly two decades. As the campaign grew, it was Keith who hired in new, trusted bodyguards to build the team responsible for protecting Trump on the trail.

Keith was always no more than an arm's length from Trump. In fact, when I first met Mr. Trump, it was Schiller who introduced me to him. As the campaign continued, Secret Service took over. What inspired me deeply through that transition was the humility of the original core that had carried us to that point. Most had to trade being in command to becoming door security. The existing staff of original bodyguards was reassigned. The only one who remained was Keith. With great humility, Schiller relinquished his position at the center of the system he'd created to protect Trump. Still, he didn't back down from the pride and responsibility he felt to defend Trump.

Those in the know were well aware Schiller was, perhaps, the most powerful man next to Trump. On the inside, it was known that when someone wanted to get a message through to Mr. Trump, it was most effectively done via Schiller.

Despite the formal titles being revoked, the original crew still had much clout with their history of boots on the ground. During the transition from campaign manager Lewandowski to Paul Manafort, I was completely cut out of the loop for a period. While I had been used to receiving my assignments from Lewandowski, his replacement, Manafort, never once contacted me. Perhaps he wanted to start fresh with his own system and crew. Maybe he thought I would take the cues to quit. Still, I remained undeterred and faithful to Trump. I was set on seeing the campaign through to the end.

At one of the first Manafort-guided events, I showed up to a fresh new media coordinator. Media Coordinator X made a point to ruffle my feathers. "What is this! What is this?" She jabbed her finger toward my chest at the campaign-issued lanyard I wore around my neck. Hung on the end of the lanyard were the credentials I'd worn for over a year that read "TRUMP Staff Photographer—Gene Ho."

For whatever reason this media coordinator had a bone to pick, and she set out to have me removed. She led me like a dog and dumped me with the man at the door. He happened to be one of Trump's original bodyguards, now in charge of event security.

"Ha! You don't know who this is?" he said. "This is Trump's longtime photographer. Gene … come on, man, follow me."

Her lowly errand boy proceeded to escort me backstage, with her tailing to verify. I wondered what important issues she was missing to follow us. Still, she trailed along, stomping to be heard.

After we'd joined the crew backstage, I looked around to see whom I knew. There stood the always-smiling Rudy Giuliani. "Hey-hey, Rudy!" For the sake of the new media coordinator, I broke my traditional protocol and went first-name basis. It emphasized my belonging. I excitedly threw in a few air punches for good measure. I was excited for my vindication.

The machine worked best as a unified force. Coordinator X proved that all the small pieces of the greater good became stronger together against her forced wedge. It was another one of those great coincidences.

Our candidate built a campaign rooted in the idea of winning. What is important to appreciate is the course he had to take for his own life. The changes Trump had to implement personally were more than any of us can ever fathom in a lifetime. The sacrifices he had to accept prove just how much he was willing to lose—*for America to win.*

Billionaire Trump was *already* winning, despite a broken America. He'd amassed a wildly successful business and estate. At age seventy, he could have more easily enjoyed these years with his grandchildren on a white sandy beach, sipping Shirley Temples. No one can argue that he deserved that.

Like Deborah, he has shown that a truly great leader is willing to relinquish reputation and glory for the overall good. He surrendered himself to lift up the American people, knowing where we go one, we go all.

If a house is divided against itself, that house cannot stand.
—spoken by Jesus in Mark 3:25

It will become all one thing, or all the other.
—Abraham Lincoln, June 16, 1858

From beginning until its end.

On right: The “first campaign rally” on April 11, 2015
in Myrtle Beach, South Carolina.

Below: To the last one held in Raleigh, North Carolina on
November 7, 2016 ...one day before the 2016 Election.

This first campaign rally in Myrtle Beach was “unofficial”
since Trump would not officially declare himself a candidate
until two months later on June 16, 2015

On the final day of the campaign,
Trump did three events over three states.
As a battleground state, North Carolina was one of them.

# Chapter 11

## Ezekiel—Future's Courier

I came to the exiles who lived at Tel Abib near the Kebar River.
And there, where they were living, I sat among them
for seven days—overwhelmed.
—Ezekiel 3:15

May 2017—Donald Trump was the president of the United States. I was six months removed from the campaign and had transitioned back to my prepolitical life.

I am a professional photographer in my twenty-sixth year. Whether it's the challenge of shooting a restaurant menu, chasing a new bride, or sitting sideline to the president of the United States, I love what I do. The most exciting aspect of my career is never feeling like I've lived the same day twice. I am awake. I am alive. I am grateful for all of it.

The older I've become, the less inclined I am to believe in coincidences. There are times you simply cannot explain away an instance with the blanket expression of coincidence. Tim Tebow's "3:16 game" is the epitome of this idea. I believe there is something divine guiding the stars. Some situations are too bizarre to have just happened. While this may or may not be one of those instances, it was quite curious with whom I shared a casual chat on this random Monday in May.

Chateau Elan, Atlanta, Georgia: I was hired to photograph an event organized for the employees of a large-scale law firm. They were to attend for work as a team-building exercise. They would kayak to understand the value of partnerships and cooperation. They would learn to face their fears via a zip-lining experience. And they would end with wine tasting at the vineyards to … well, maybe that part was to serve itself.

On this final day of the conference, I stood in the atrium running through the last-minute details. In a moment, our special guest speaker would join us. That guest speaker just happened to be Tony Schwartz, coauthor of Trump's *The Art of the Deal*.

The connection had nothing to do with Trump and me. This company had desired a motivational speaker to inspire their employees, so they hired Tony Schwartz. They wanted a photographer to cover the events, so they hired Gene Ho. It was purely coincidence—if you don't question that sort of thing.

I showed up early, hoping I might stumble across Schwartz before the talk. There I found him sitting alone, quietly thumbing through his cell phone outside the conference hall. It was a bit unnerving to approach him. There had (and continues to be) a rather public quarrel between Tony Schwartz and Donald Trump. In fact, Schwartz had been quite vocal in his opposition.

I eased in with familiar niceties. I introduced myself as the photographer for the event at which he would be speaking. We had a quaint conversation about the weather. We shared where we were from, what we'd done while in Atlanta, and bits about our families. About fifteen minutes into the conversation, I jumped in with both feet. It was the Luke Skywalker moment: "Tony, I am your father." No, but the confession felt just as epic.

"Tony, you're not going to believe this, but I was Trump's campaign photographer for two years." I was hopeful he wouldn't end the conversation right then and there. Thankfully, he didn't. For a moment, though, he looked as though he was being punked. I laughed (probably uncomfortably) and expressed that although I was a Trump supporter, his deal with Trump was his deal. As deplorables, we knew that not everyone thought Trump hung the moon.

Even after the unexpected revelation, we continued a great conversation. Admittedly, Tony Schwartz was not at all what I expected. I had a preconceived idea of his personality since I had read *The Art of the Deal*. It is a dynamic read, powerfully written and authoritative. For these qualities, I expected him to be an intense figure. Yet Tony Schwartz, sitting before me, was so docile. Again I was reminded people are not defined wholly by the thing we revere them for.

The exchange between us was reminiscent of the previous two years for me. On the campaign trail, I had rubbed elbows with so many engaging and unique individuals. Now, as chance would have it, I was face-to-face with the coauthor of one of the most legendary Donald Trump reads in history. Meanwhile I was personally hen-scratching my own Trump hardback. Granted, 90 percent of humanity seems to be.

To meet someone in person gives you a new perspective. You no longer rely on the idea of the person that your mind created. A quick study of Tony's biography tells you he grew up in a household centered on big business and big ideas. His mother created a nonprofit in the 1960s that is at a global level today. Naturally, he followed the path his mother pounded out as a philanthropist, author, and advocate.

Tony had sat in my company, so reserved and unassuming. Mere moments later, he exploded onto the stage. It was as though he were a different man entirely. I was shocked at his intensity level. He turned on and went from zero to one hundred. Ironically, Schwartz's talk that day centered a lot on performance, endurance, and energy. With the insider's peek I'd had, I felt I had the best vantage point to appreciate the sentiment.

Donald Trump or Tony Schwartz might not be keen to hear it, but they are similar in at least one respect: energy. I saw firsthand how these two individuals (at sixty-five-plus years of age) took a dynamic presence to the stage.

There is a man in the Bible who was similar. Ezekiel was known for his engaging performances and unrestrained methods for conveying his messages.

**Meet Ezekiel**

Ezekiel is one of the bigger books in the Bible. While not an everyday favorite, Ezekiel not only is interesting but also has a strong message to share.

About twenty-six hundred years ago, Ezekiel was commissioned by God to deliver a message. He was to document the Lord's words and be sure that all he had been shown was made known. What makes this story so relevant now is for whom the message was to be delivered. The message Ezekiel was to share was meant for someone he would never meet, far into the future and long after his death.

The story began in 600 BC when King Nebuchadnezzar sent the Babylonian army to storm the House of Judah. Raiders from the east came to trample the territory, demanding tribute (imagine, more "taxes"). After the Babylonian army succeeded in the takeover, the victors began to deport large groups of people. Ezekiel, a young Jew of just twenty-five years of age, was among them. It was in this time of captivity that God called Ezekiel to become a prophet in Babylon.

Ezekiel wasn't the picture of a man one might envision as a prophetic minister of the word of God. One visualized a prophet as a bearded old man, stoic and strained, wearing a robe and carrying a stone tablet. Ezekiel is further proof God chooses whom He sees fit. Ezekiel was known for outlandish antics and unusual tactics to draw attention to his message. Those unorthodox ways helped his words spread like wildfire.

An example of one of his unconventional performances was his mock battlefield. He created a miniature version of the city of Jerusalem. Like a child playing with little green army men, he publicly created a detailed spectacle of the siege on Jerusalem. Ezekiel bombarded the replica city, which was surrounded by enemy camps, with tiny battering rams. He quickly gained a reputation for his energetic displays.

Another unusual method of delivery showed Ezekiel's commitment to his objective. For 390 days he lay, bound and tied, on his left side. He did so to demonstrate the length of time necessary to bear the sins of the unruly House of Israel. Then he turned to his right side, and he lay forty days for the House of Judah. As God demanded—a day for each year.

For the sake of appreciating this feat, attempt to finish reading this chapter without jostling in your seat. Wide awake, Ezekiel remained bound and restrained as he watched the world go by. The demonstration lasted a year and two months. Meanwhile we've not finished the paragraph and already have readjusted for comfort.

God asked that Ezekiel use any means necessary to wake the people of Israel and bring them back to Him. God does not wish to remain a vague, far-off concept, lost in the cosmos of man-made fiction. He knew there would be a time we could be lost in it. So He gave us His Son and called Him the Truth. He wants us to know Him, to love Him, and to serve Him—without compromise.

The message Ezekiel was charged to carry is for you.

And he said to me, "Son of man, eat what is before you, eat this scroll; then go and speak to the house of Israel." So I opened my mouth and he gave me the scroll to eat.

—Ezekiel 3:1–2

There are a few aspects of our past that must be discussed in order to understand to whom he was speaking. The House of Israel is not confined to a tiny Middle Eastern state that borders the Mediterranean Sea. Let me explain:

God loved Abraham. Abraham was promised that his descendants would multiply throughout the land—to the north, south, east, and west. He promised those descendants would be as numerous as the stars in the sky and the sands on the seashore. Abraham was the original father of all who believe in God's word. Muslims follow God's word through Ishmael, son of Abraham. Christians follow God's word through Isaac, son of Abraham.

Abraham > Isaac > Jacob

Jacob was Abraham's grandson, blessed beyond measure and beloved by God. Note Genesis, where God speaks to Jacob:

> Your name will no longer be Jacob, but Israel,
> because you have struggled with God and with men
> and have overcome.
> —Genesis 32:28

When we reference the House of Israel or the House of Judah, we are speaking of the sons of Jacob (aka Israel). Jacob fathered twelve sons, known as the twelve tribes of Israel.

We tend to think the blessed children of Abraham were all Jews. However, of the twelve tribes, only *some* of them were Jewish. Think of it this way: those born in Texas are Americans, but not all Americans are Texans. The same idea can apply here. Indeed, the Jews were Israelites, but not all the tribes of Israel were Jewish. They were a part of the whole.

The scroll that Ezekiel was asked to swallow looked inedible. The words held within were strewn with lament, mourning, and woe—a forewarning. He did as he was asked, and he swallowed the scroll. To his surprise, the words were as sweet as honey. Upon consuming the scroll, the Lord then commanded Ezekiel to take those words to the House of Israel. Be warned, He said, they are stubborn and may not listen to you. However hardheaded they could be, God promised to make Ezekiel just as much so.

As He promised, the sons of Jacob flourished and multiplied and spread to all four corners of the earth. Much of the movement was westward into Europe and subsequently the United States. You might consider Ezekiel's warning was meant for delivery to your own front door.

Ezekiel preached virtually nonstop for a span of nearly thirty years. He was high energy and uniquely memorable in drawing attention to his message. He was the great performing artist of his time, and his teaching methods were bizarre and a little outrageous.

It was easy to strike the comparison between the energetic showmanship of Ezekiel and that of Donald Trump. Trump is a man who does everything "bigly." His uniquely animated gestures are off the beaten path. Trump's distinctive hair has been discussed at length, and there are more memes featuring his offbeat facial expressions than we could count.

With his over-the-top theatrics and unbridled energy, Donald Trump drew the watchful eyes of the world. In large part, that unique flare and intensity garnered him the attention he received. The result was that his message reached your ears. Much like Ezekiel's showmanship, Trump has allowed his to do the same.

### Enter Trump

Early in the campaign, someone who had known Trump better than I did said that he only slept three hours a night. It was unbelievable. It almost sounded like a public relations ploy, or an urban legend, created to imply how hard Trump worked. It seemed superhuman, impossible that this was true.

After watching him in action over the course of two years, however, if there was anyone I could believe this to be true of … it would be Trump.

As I watched, I found that he was very much like Ezekiel. After God revealed himself to Ezekiel for the first time, he took seven days to absorb what he had seen. He was utterly shell-shocked:

> I came to the exiles who lived at Tel Abib near the Kebar River. And there, where they were living, I sat among them for seven days—overwhelmed.
> —Ezekiel 3:15

One of the early, more largely attended rallies that Trump delivered left me with a memory I'll never forget. While he wasn't doing the massive arena speeches yet, he had outgrown the fifty-people-in-a-room talks. Trump was no stranger to speaking to huge crowds. However, this event came with added personal pressure since it was Trump only. Also, for the first time, the press was there in suffocating force.

Trump was the only candidate—probably in history—who routinely had the press live streaming and broadcasting his rally speeches. Because of this, Trump had to stay fresh. He began to reinvent his speech from event to event. This added one more thread of difficulty to Trump's campaign compared to his rivals. To remaster the talking points each time to stay engaging was no small feat. This was especially so for a man traveling to numerous events, even in a single day. Still Trump figured this out early and adjusted accordingly.

On this day, Trump delivered his talk to an estimated two thousand in attendance. This was a huge number at the time. Even at the peak of other candidates' campaigns, they were lucky to see half that number at a single event. His delivery was epic, as if he was fueled by the energy of the larger crowd. He was intense and concise, with his usual comedic charm.

Following the talk, he left the stage, and we walked the halls back to his "green room." I emphasize with quotes because it wasn't exactly the high-class green room you're picturing. In smaller venues, we would make due with conference halls or meeting rooms. They converted what was available to provide a sanctuary for the speakers. It was a comfortable little room, one with retractable walls to adjust to a suitable size. The room was mostly bare, nothing too fancy, but the tables were draped in cloth, and refreshments were available.

Once the door of the room closed behind us, Trump gave an audible sigh of relief. He picked up a bottle of water, opened the lid, and washed his hands with it. Then he leaned forward and used the water left on his hands to wash the sweat from his face. He reached for the available loose end of a tablecloth, and he dried his face.

I stood in awe. The man who I had seen as a seemingly indestructible force for months appeared so raw and human in that moment. Until that moment, everything I'd seen seemed like it came from a bottomless energy source. In this unedited act, I was reminded immediately who stood before me: a man. He is just a man. He sweats, he bleeds, and he's flawed.

Mostly I loved how real that moment was. It was relatable. When I was a teenager, I was dining with an older cousin. At the end of dinner, I needed to rinse my hands. Rather than excusing myself to use the washroom, I dipped my fingers into the glass of water in front of me. My cousin looked at me, shook his head in disappointment, and suggested, "It's ice water, so there's condensation. Next time just rub the side of the glass." My name is Gene, but I've never claimed to be a genius.

My point is Trump knows table-side decorum. This was his event, his green room, with his tablecloth. He had just given one of the best talks of his campaign, and he was exhausted. Sitting before me, in a quiet moment alone, he demonstrated the age-old truth, "Never let them see you sweat."

It endeared me to him to see Trump so genuine. As a photographer, I've given lectures in front of groups of nearly a thousand people. I've spoken in Vegas at the professional photographers' convention, and in New York for my sponsors. Few people would know that I dry heave before all my talks.

Watching Trump, it's clear that he possesses tremendous energy. What I had an opportunity to see was just how much that energy costs. He was drained. Yet, not even fifteen minutes later, Trump emerged from that same green room back to being Trump. Out of sight, he had gathered himself. When he came out of that room, he was reinvigorated. Just a few moments of peace had restored him to the electric storm we'd come to expect.

This event was before the Secret Service had been introduced. So the VIP group he was to greet wasn't a limited line like the Secret Service later dictated. The VIP room was bustling with a lively group, networking and shaking hands. Trump went in and worked the room. After about thirty sporadic VIP photos, one of the staffers charged me to wrap it up.

Trump had been given the "escape route" by the organizing staff, yet he replied, "Not yet. Let's get a group picture!" This moment became one of my favorite photos from the campaign. I loved this image for two reasons, the first being the excitement level of the supporters. The crowd in that room was so enthused that Trump remained past the clock, and they huddled around him. It was reminiscent of a group of old college friends as they piled in for a quick snapshot. It was a product of the times, which is the second reason I loved this photo. While I took it, I thought this could very well be the last time that *this* picture would happen. And, at least from what I saw, it was.

While there was a time when people could swarm Trump, the sun has set on that day. After the introduction of Secret Service, this would likely never again happen in his lifetime. Secret Service could never allow so many unverified people around him for a group shot like this.

As Trump left that day, he was met by a highly decorated veteran in a wheelchair. Trump always made sure to give special recognition to our armed forces and expressed such appreciation for our veterans. Amid the chaotic bottleneck of everyone exiting the VIP room, Trump stopped to speak with this man. As I fumbled my way through the sea of people behind him, Trump yelled over his shoulder and waved to me. "Photographer!"

Yes … that was me. Not Gene Ho. Not Gene, but "photographer." My name is Gene, but my title was enough to validate that I had a place in it.

****

I often stop to reflect on the amazing people I've met in my life and how they've come to the top. I try to wrap my head around the core lessons our Bible shares with us in hopes I might learn from them. I read the stories of divinity and greatness, and it's hard not to feel like I fall short sometimes. Then I'm reminded that not one man alive was/is/will be perfect, except One. More freeing still is to remember that He is on my team.

People do accomplish extraordinary things. There are individuals who are worthy of our inspiration and those we may seek to model ourselves after. But at the end of the day, they are still human like you and me. Perhaps some of their success can be credited to an advanced application of the principles God has shared with us. What's more, perhaps it's not even necessary to realize the motivation for Him when we do.

Like Ezekiel and Trump, we can apply the same principles for our lives. We are born to succeed by using our God-given strengths. Quirky and unique as they are, Ezekiel and Trump prove success can be found in embracing the value of who we are.

So he became... the President of the United States of America, Donald J. Trump

What an honor it was to witness history as I did.

Here, President Trump is flanked by the American Flag and the Flag of the President of the United States.

The night before the election, I gave my personal endorsement
and public support to Trump by means of my personal social media.

I had held off two years making a profession for my conviction.
I wanted my word to be trustworthy and true.
After two years watching him in action, both on and off
the public stage, I was confident in the words I shared.

This was our man.

# Chapter 12

### Didymus

I will never believe.

—spoken by Didymus in John 20:25

I love boxing. I like to pair myself up with what would be my weight class. Then I imagine, with the right shift in my path, I'd be in the ring tearing it up. I have to admit, boxing is a great sport to enjoy vicariously through someone else because it's that person's face—and not yours.

I enjoy the strategy involved and can appreciate the amount of physical dedication it would take to train to that level. But what I love most about boxing is that walk into the ring! It allows so much imagination into the personality of the individual joining the fight. Obviously the objective is to be as intimidating as possible. It's an opportunity to strike fear into the opponent and the boxer's fans. It never ceases to amaze me that some of the most menacing are uncharacteristically serene and composed. I love the sport and its presentation.

A large part of why I enjoy it is for the same reason I enjoy a lot of things: I love to people watch. It's a way to let your mind invent the plot of what could be someone's story. It's also a way to sit in the mall, watch from afar, and consider the couple across the food court. How long have they been together? What might they be shopping for? What do they do for a living? The possibilities of curiosity are endless. The chances of being right are maybe impossible, but it's a wonderfully inventive way to pass the time.

I also love boxing because of its insight into how people face adversity. There are old videos that feature a young Mike Tyson crying before he entered the ring. Years later, when Tyson became a wrecking machine and held the title of heavyweight world champion, he confessed how nervous he was before a fight. But, he said, the closer he got to the ring, the more fiercely confident he became.

It's hard to fathom the commitment it would take to train for a boxing match. Besides the endless sparing, the cardio, and the diet required, consider the twisted mind games you would have to subject yourself to. On one hand, you'd have to constantly convince yourself that you were going to win and that you're unstoppable. At the same time, to push yourself to new limits, you would also need to experience failure. The winners push themselves to lose in practice, and that inevitably creates an avenue for doubt.

Doubt has always had a negative connotation, but doubt can be an incredible motivator and deserves credit for its role in the good as well.

Take Erin Brockovich, for example. The unemployed mother of three was skeptical enough to believe the PG&E water company in Hinkley, California, had poisoned the water supply and covered it up. It was because of her mistrust in the system that the company was exposed for covering up years of fatal pollutants. The case resulted in the largest settlement ever paid in a direct-action lawsuit in US history.

Doubt can be productive. It causes a chain reaction of critical thinking. Doubt can push you to consider alternative routes. Doubt insists on independent analysis.

I have never been a boxer, nor have I been responsible for exposing a company's large-scale corruption. One thing I have experienced is business. Truthfully, I'm not very good at it. Photography is a horrible career if you're out to make mountains of cash. I've survived the years with a smile, but there are far better ways to make bank.

As far as photographers go, I've earned some accolades along the way. I've photographed the president of the United States. My portfolio of clients looks like a who's who of sports, politics, and Hollywood. Over the course of my career, I've probably shot close to fifteen hundred weddings. Yet I'm richer with stories than I am with wealth. I'm average at best when it comes to business.

When I started my company, I had already been in the photography industry for a few years. Starting any business is a struggle, and I was barely making ends meet. At twenty-five years old, my mom came to visit me. As Chinese mothers do, she laid it out in black and white. I had one more year. When the year was up, if the "photography thing" hadn't worked itself out, it would be time to get a real job.

I will never forget that conversation. I love photography, and it stung to hear her criticisms. I'd finally found something that I *wanted* to do. She's older and wiser, and ultimately, I knew she had my best interest at heart. For as hard as it was to hear, I knew she was right.

I began to convince myself that I was doing well. Each job I took, I chose to believe *this* would be the job that would lead to the next big break. This wasn't so much faith in my photography skills or me as much as it was convincing myself to believe it.

Faith takes work, and it means trusting sometimes blindly. The choice of what to believe is yours. We should all remember that we don't always have to see the air we breathe to know it's filling our lungs.

There are few stronger examples of faith in the Bible than this one. Introducing the apostle Didymus.

**Meet Didymus**

Within this book we've covered twelve people from the Bible. Some of their stories crossed paths; some were relatives or descendants. With some we can easily relate, or like Ruth, some are people we aspire to be like. Some of the stories are beautiful accounts of integrity, while others are shockingly sinister. One thing I'd like to note is not all the selected individuals were working for the interest of God, but they still leave us with plenty to think about and learn from.

Of the twelve featured in this book, Didymus is the only one from the New Testament. This wasn't done purposely. It came as it did.

I believe we are given this life with purpose, and we should walk in the light by which we feel led. I implore you to seek answers, to find truth. I've challenged myself over the years to unravel the words, separate of a governing body. I can't take credit or call myself brave; it wasn't a path I chose for myself. The church I belonged to had put me in exile. It was a case where doubt was a great thing, and it arrived when least expected. I consider myself lucky that I chose to doubt man and the establishment, instead of doubting my God.

It is of the utmost importance that when you search for truth, you do so without judgment or venom. There is only one God, our Lord, YHWH. Most all religions boil down to this collective understanding. The frustration often stems from a lack of cognizance, and we project our fears, repeating the bumper-sticker phrases that come easily.

Dig deeper, beyond repeating casual phrases, and make them who you are. Everything you need to find peace is in front of you, but you need to open your eyes to see it:

> Get rid of all bitterness, rage and anger, brawling and slander, along with every form of malice. Be kind and compassionate to one another, forgiving each other, just as in Christ God forgave you.
> —Ephesians 4:31–32

In this book, I've talked about Christian events. I also touched on a few Jewish events from the Torah. (The Torah is comprised of the first five books of the Old Testament.) If you want to go further, many of the people featured here are descendants of Abraham—meaning they are cousins to Ishmael. Ishmael's descendants founded the Muslim faith. Ultimately everything is connected at the core, and we are all for God.

I face this subject with Didymus because there are both good and bad people whose stories were noted in the Bible. There are some foul individuals who have honorable qualities, and there are some wonderful people who acted shamefully. We can learn from both instances.

When it comes to Didymus, I feel compelled to defend his legacy. He is a good man with a bad rap. I've struggled to reconcile the perception of King Solomon and that of Didymus.

Let's give this book a little meat and add some adventure into the tell-all you've been waiting for. Here's a little exposé on King Solomon, a man who is still revered today. He is ingrained in our minds as a pillar of faith and unparalleled wisdom. He is celebrated at children's Bible camp. Yet he died unfaithful with more than a few skeletons in his closet. Meanwhile someone with true faith, Didymus, ended up with a slanderous nickname like "Doubting Thomas." The prevailing notion was that he was a bad example of true Christian faith.

So maybe we can untwist the reasoning and redeem the apostle Thomas.

King Solomon first:

Solomon was one of King David's sons. Upon David's death he was given the throne and offered a gift from God. He asked for wisdom, and he received it in abundance.

King Solomon was greater in riches and wisdom than all the other kings
of the earth. The whole world sought audience with Solomon
to hear the wisdom God had put in his heart.
—1 Kings 10:23, 24

Solomon is best known for his wisdom through the story of the two women and the baby. Two women in the kingdom had shared a home; each had given birth to a baby boy just three days apart. The mother of one of the babies accidentally smothered her son while sleeping. In the night she crept to her roommate's bedside and took the live baby and replaced him with her deceased child.

When they woke, an argument ensued, and they took their issue before the king. Both women insisted the living infant to be her own. King Solomon declared, "Bring me a sword." Then he gave the order to cut the child in two, giving half to each woman. The first woman shrieked in horror and insisted the baby be given to the other, and the second woman agreed this to be an acceptable resolve. The truth stood before him, and he released the baby to his rightful mother—the woman who could not allow him die, no matter the cost.

Solomon was wise. That is not in dispute. I only question the admiration he still carries today. Solomon had lost favor in the eyes of God. Ultimately, Solomon was given anything his heart desired in exchange for his end of the bargain: God asked that he walk with integrity of heart. This was a promise Solomon did not keep. Ironically Solomon's deepest struggle stems from a verse, I believe, that is also often misinterpreted. God asked Solomon not to intermarry with the women of other nations. (This is a fragment of the whole.) God didn't stop there; he explained why: *because they would turn his heart after their evil gods.* There are two teams here: the team for God and those with an agenda against Him.

This was a warning. It was no different from the advice to choose your friends wisely. You are the company you keep. Returning this fragment to its context, God said, "Don't marry someone who murders people." It's sound advice. Solomon's lack of taking this simple advice explains his downfall.

Solomon kept seven hundred wives and three hundred concubines, and his detestable wives led him astray. Solomon erected places of worship to Moloch, the god of child sacrifice, and Chemosh, another deity known for human sacrifice. Also calling to question his character and loyalties, Solomon was responsible for setting his own salary. The salary King Solomon had selected for himself was telling:

> Now the weight of gold that came to Solomon in one year was 666 talents of gold.
> —1 Kings 10:14

I find it worth noting that upon being elected president of the United States, Donald Trump set his annual salary at zero dollars. Mr. Trump has donated 100 percent of his presidential salary to charity. Trump was also noted in *Forbes* for being "the most notable loser" on its list of the four hundred wealthiest Americans. According to the report, in his first year of presidency, he personally lost over $600 million. So we are living in the times of a man who gave an oath to lead our country. Trump is fulfilling that promise, not only for free but also at great financial loss. Still he is demonized. Yet Solomon, the celebrated saint, requested a paycheck in the number of the beast. I don't think the number he chose was an accident.

In contrast, in one of the greatest shows of faith, Didymus, otherwise known as Doubting Thomas, was resigned to being referenced as one with little faith. Somewhere in time he made his way into Bible lore as a weak man. Nowhere in the good book was he called for failure. Never was he biblically referred to as Doubting Thomas.

I argue Thomas was, in fact, a great man of faith. Thomas was one of the twelve apostles of Jesus Christ. Of the twelve, Thomas was quite possibly the one with the greatest faith of all. The story of Lazarus is a great example of Thomas's dedication and unwavering loyalty to Jesus. A dear friend of Jesus was very ill. Jesus explained to His disciples that they must go to be with His friend Lazarus, as he had fallen asleep. His disciples thought better of it and asked that they not go to Lazarus in Judea. The last time Jesus had been there the Jews tried to stone Him. However, they had misunderstood Jesus's words. He spoke more clearly:

> Then Jesus said to them plainly, "Lazarus is dead. And I am glad
> for your sakes that I was not there, that you may believe.
> Nevertheless let us go to him."
> Then Thomas (called Didymus) said to the rest of the
> disciples, "Let us go, that we may die with him."
> —John 11:14–16

There are two important lessons here. The first: While eleven of the twelve apostles were coaxing Jesus not to go, Thomas spoke up. He was willing to go even if that meant dying. His faith and conviction in Jesus was so great that death would not stop him from following.

The second point: Let me reiterate, Jesus was glad that He would have an opportunity to give them *more* reason to believe. He wanted to *show* them for themselves, so they would have every reason to stand firm in their faith. He wasn't asking that they believe it secondhand. Physically, in their presence, He was willing to give them more.

Lazarus had been dead for four days, with a stone in front of his tomb. Jesus asked the stone to be removed. Hesitantly they did so. Jesus asked our Father to hear His prayer for the sake of those in attendance, so they may believe. He asked God to bring Lazarus back from death. And He did.

****

After Jesus's death and resurrection, He returned to the apostles. Thomas was the only one who hadn't been there to see Jesus upon His return. Though the eleven recounted the experience, Thomas doubted that Jesus lived again. He wanted what his friends had—to see his friend Jesus for himself.

Jesus did appear to him and gave us a message. "Because you have seen me, you have believed; blessed are those who have not seen and yet still believe."

Thomas was the representation of us today. Though we didn't live to see with our own eyes, it is the lesson Jesus shared with Thomas that is more valuable than anything that came before it.

Without the risk of doubt, how much value can be of faith?

**Enter Trump**

Trump is the ultimate self-promoter. He has the power of persuasion. He can convince you that he can do the impossible and is world-renowned for his supreme confidence.

Treat the word *impossible* as nothing more than motivation.
—Donald Trump

Of this, there is no need for me to convince you. There were more than a handful of television interviews, rallies, and commercials where Trump publicly unleashed his bravado.

It reminds me a lot of the "rice experiment." A few years back, Dr. Masaru Emoto, a Japanese scientist, performed a series of experiments to prove his theories. His belief was that the power of our willful thinking and intentions can manifest tangible results.

A resulting experiment started with three separate jars. Each jar was sanitized and prepared in identical fashion. A pot of rice was cooked, and equal amounts of it were placed into each of the three jars. After being tightly sealed, each jar was labeled—one with "love," one with "hate," and the last with "ignore." For the weeks and months that followed, each jar would be subject to its namesake. Love rice was praised and adored, the hate rice was a verbal catchall, and ignore rice sat unattended. The only difference for each of these nonliving items was the change in the projection of its "captor's" willful intention.

Since this is something any regular Joe can do in his own home, many have repeated the process. (Granted this isn't under intense laboratory conditions.) A reasonable amount of consistency can be achieved, and numerous trials can be attempted. The results are shockingly similar across the board. Ignored rice shows some discoloration but is not dramatically changed. Hate rice becomes a battlefield of mold, and love looks good enough to eat. Love rice appears like the same fluffy grains as day one.

A good man brings good things out of the good stored in his heart and
an evil man brings evil things out of the evil stored up in his heart.
For the mouth speaks what the heart is full of.
—Luke 6:45

We don't give enough credit to the power of positive, willful consciousness. I believe, through the power of positivity, Mr. Trump was able to command a collective confidence that was contagious. Your perception and projection into the world can bring you both positive and negative energy. It's a very real thing, and it works both ways.

Years ago, I had a friend who may have needed a teensy pinch of work on his projection. It was midsummer on the beach with ninety-degree temperatures. He strolled up the street to snag a bottle of water from the vending machine. He returned shortly after in a flurry of expletives with a rock-solid block of Aquafina in hand. Highly amused, another friend went to the machine, pressed the same button, and returned with a regular, not-so-entertaining bottle of water. Now irate, he stormed up the street with another dollar bill. If it weren't for three witnesses, no one would believe it … The machine dispensed him *yet another frozen-to-the-core bottle of water.*

So here's the thing. Do you think for a second that Trump set out to be president of the United States and never had doubts? As sure as he is human, he did. I was there. I witnessed it personally.

What's ironic is that the rabid media never picked up on some of these comments. They were far more interested in taking the sound bites that worked to show him as an egomaniac: "I love winning! I always win. We will have so much winning when I'm elected you'll get bored with winning!"

Distortions. We saw what the media wanted us to see. This is similar to how we are shown Solomon as a worthy role model and beloved prophet, but Thomas's legacy portrays him a failure.

Trump had doubts. In times of question, he fell on the faith of his family. It was through the encouragement of his wife and children that he grew to believe he could achieve what he has. In more than one interview, various members of his family are heard saying that they knew once he set his mind to doing it, he would win.

What more does a man need to convince himself that he can
than the unshakable faith of his family telling him that *he will*?

If you can believe it, there was a time the media wasn't hanging on Trump's every word. I was there. In one of his early speeches, Trump finished his talk and opened the floor, asking, "Any questions?" While Trump wasn't yet a candidate, he had mentioned *thinking* of running. One person there posed this question: "Donald, what would happen if you ran for president and you didn't win?"

At the time, next to no one considered him a viable candidate. This was the "he can't be serious" and "this is a stunt" era. It was wonderful that a citizen posed this question, poetically averting the gnarly jaws of the mainstream media. Genuinely Trump replied, "If I run and I don't win? Then I'll just go back to doing what I'm doing, and I'll just ride off into the sunset."

I remember that so distinctly because I thought he would respond differently. I had even hoped he would respond differently. I was ready to see ultimate confidence. As a seemingly lone supporter, well ahead of the masses, I almost *needed* Trump to show some grit.

Trump had doubts. He just chose not to project them for public consumption. His campaign and subsequent presidency had/have had more opposition and attempts at character assassination than any other in history. Granted, *some* of it was a product of his own missteps. I was there. When Trump had to backpedal on the McCain/war hero fiasco, I was there. After the leaked "locker-room" tapes, I was there. We weren't naive. We knew the gravity. And so did he.

For as many times as I had professed confidently that I knew he would win, there were ten conversations in my head debating how. Perhaps inside all of us is the same power of persuasion Trump touts.

The funny thing about doubt is you can't control its comings and goings. But faith is stronger than doubt because *you control faith*.

To be fair, some of us who believed Trump could take the presidency believed out of desperation. The economy, our security, the future of our nation—so much was at stake, more than ever before in our history. He said things we didn't really want to hear but knew were true. He didn't have all the answers, but the fiery passion he had in what he believed was evident. We, the silent majority, knew America could not bear another round of the same.

Donald Trump might not have been the perfect candidate, but he was ours. He took to the podium, with a mic and the gumption, to give us the gross, honest truth. It was raw and unpolished. And in those glorious flaws came a truth that unraveled while we were waking:

A flawed man fighting for what's right
is any man fighting for what's right.

Monday, November 7, 2016, the day before the general election—Everybody in the arena knew we were on the cusp of great change. We knew we had won. Ironically, at the time, we had no idea how much.

Election Day 2016—My work was done. My family nestled in for the night, preparing for our celebration. My wife bought glittered champagne flutes for the children, and we poured them each a glass of sparkling grape juice. Over the celebratory cheers, I knew they could not yet understand how this day was a milestone that changed the landscape of history. I thanked God for all the forks in the road. Each one had led me here, where I belonged. I was home.

Don't be ashamed to doubt. Jesus understood that Didymus needed His reassurance to believe for himself. Jesus gave many miraculous signs in the presence of His disciples, and they are written within the Bible so you may believe. If the words seem too distant, truly open your heart and ask. He's been right upstairs, waiting. The floor is yours.

# Conclusion

Apocalypse: ἀποκάλυψις, "an uncovering, revealing, or unveiling."

From *Strong's Concordance*:
An apocalypse is a disclosure of knowledge or revelation.
In religious contexts it is usually a disclosure of something hidden,
"a vision of heavenly secrets that can make sense of earthly realities."

•••••••••••••••••••••••••••••••••••••••••••••••••••••••••••••

I sat down on the night of the 2016 election with my head reeling.
We had accomplished what we'd set out to do. It was finished.

As the days and weeks passed, friends and colleagues asked
what was to become of me.
I never could have known the adventure that would begin
within the walls of my own home and within my heart.

I sat down planning to decompress.
What began as a cathartic release of personal memoirs
slowly evolved into something entirely of its own making.
This venture began with a personal title—*Trumpographer*.
It embodied me: the man, the camera, the chase.

As the weeks went by, it became clear that it wasn't about me.
The title that emboldened my part in it seemed inaccurate.

I was only a small observer to part of the whole.
So the title became more appropriately developed into action:
*Trumpography.*

An action is something that can be observed and implemented.
It turned the focus to where I thought it more appropriate:
to Donald Trump, our president.

Until recently.
As the pages continued to write themselves,
and a thing that took on a life of its own stared back at me,
the revelation became perfectly obvious:
This isn't about Donald Trump either.

Donald J. Trump was merely the catalyst of opportunity.
He was the vehicle provided in my path to drive attention to where it
truly belongs: to the word of the Lord.

God has big plans underway.

America has struggled to appreciate President Trump,
while Israel has minted a temple coin with
Donald Trump's profile flanking that of Cyrus.

There have been so many articles and blogs written, drawing the
parallels between the life of Cyrus and that of Trump,
that the mainstream media has penned rebuttals.
An American Cyrus, they laugh.
Poor, desperate Christians, they say.
As though it's too absurd a possibility that, perhaps, history repeats itself.

It's easier to believe each day is an adventure.

No one wants to feel powerless to the idea that perhaps
the story has already been written.

My friends, it has.
You have the free will to choose your path.
But don't think for a second that God is surprised by your choice
when you choose it.

****

It is merely coincidence
that Isaiah 45 tells the story of a life
quite like that of our forty-fifth president.
The story of Cyrus, a man who was being used by God
though he did not acknowledge Him.

It is also a coincidence that the number seven
is the foundation for God's word.

Seven is used hundreds of times throughout the Bible.

From Jesus's seven "I am"s,
seven days of creation to completion,
and the final days of Revelation
through the 7 seals, 7 angels, and 7 trumpets.

Perhaps it is also by coincidence then
that Donald Trump was born June 14, 1946,
and took his seat as president of the United States of America
on January 20, 2017.
Purely coincidence, on that day,
he became the oldest president in history to take office

at 70 years, 7 months, and 7 days.

****

I'm not totally convinced of coincidence.

A dear Greek friend shined light on my feelings when
we discussed the topic together recently.
*Coincidence*, translated from the Greek word *synkirion*, means
"Together with supreme authority."

She stressed this word was only used in reference to the divine.

A biblical definition then would be
"an occurrence by God's chosen arrangement of circumstances."
Under this idea,
coincidence, in relation to the idea there are no coincidences,
leaves it as God's hand.
The fact of the matter is
it's for each of us to see through the confusion
and make our own deductions of what to believe.

Question the narrative, do your research; find your own truth.

As Christians we are brought up to be meek,
fearing our own voice and questioning our own value before God.

We file into church on Sunday
seeking the wisdom of the one in the robe.
We seek God's forgiveness and understanding through a third-party middleman.
Nowhere in the Bible does God charge you to schedule Him
only on Sunday, for only one hour.

Quite the opposite; God asks that when you seek Him,
go to your room and close the door,
for your conversations with Him are between your heart and His.

*And when you pray, do not be like the hypocrites,*
*for they love to pray standing in the synagogues and on the street corners*
*to be seen by men.*
*I tell you the truth, they have received their reward in full.*
*But when you pray, go into your room, close the door and pray to*
*your Father, who sees what is done in secret, will reward you.*
—Matthew 6:5–6

I'm not suggesting that we stop attending church.
But for so many, we already have.
His believers have been divided into hundreds of denominations,
slowly driving a wedge between us.

Rest assured the opposition is solidly united.

This is war. It always has been. To the victor go the spoils.
And you, my friends, are the goods to be won.
The war is for you.

See, they've had you believe the world is so big, the universe so expansive,
you could never understand.
They'd like you to continue to believe
you are insignificant and unworthy.
A forced division between you and Our Father.
But He says, not only are you enough – you are *everything*.

****

I have used this platform as an opportunity to help open our eyes,
to see that God may choose an unlikely candidate,
and to prove to you that He already has:

In Jonah, a man who ran from Him;
Rahab, a prostitute with a scarlet cord;
or Didymus, a prophet who'd witnessed miracles displayed
before his own eyes yet needed just a *little* more help to believe.

*Brothers, think of what you were when you were called.*
*Not many of you were wise by human standards;*
*not many were influential; not many were of noble birth.*
*But God chose the foolish things of the world to shame the wise;*
*God chose the weak things of the world to shame the strong.*
*He chose the lowly things of the world and the despised things*
*—and the things that are not—*
*to nullify the things that are.*
—1 Corinthians 26–28

Don't let the ugliness of the world close out your worth
when you possess the power to make the world better,
in your action.
Don't let the world's perceived enormity convince you
to willfully silence your voice.
Fight. Fight. Fight.

He's given you the living Word, the Holy Bible, the sword, and the shield,
which means He offers you the protection needed
in times of offense and those of defense.

Break free from the monotonous routines we've carved for ourselves.
God is calling us to lift up our faces.

He will give opportunity after opportunity to see Him.
Be mindful:
You can't see what you're not looking for,
you can't hear if you're not listening,
and you can't receive what you don't ask Him for.

*Ask and it will be given to you;*
*seek and you will find;*
*knock and the door will be opened to you.*
*For everyone who asks receives; he who seeks finds;*
*and to him who knocks, the door will be opened.*
—Matthew 7:7–8

We have a job to do.
Each one of us is capable of contributing something
unique & beautiful.
It's time to do better.
For our children.

It's time to think independently.
Research.
Expand your thinking.
Lift the veil.

Remember the majority is going to be wrong.
This is about the remnant, the broken, and the despised.
We the people, the silent majority, the sleeping giant … is waking.

****

Perhaps it is simply another coincidence that you have read these words,
history merged with the present

as seen through the eyes of a wedding photographer:

*I saw the Holy City, the new Jerusalem,*
*coming down out of heaven from God,*
*prepared as a bride beautifully dressed for her husband …*
*Then he said, "write this down,*
*for these words are trustworthy and true."*
—Revelation 21:2–5

Or maybe it's an opportunity.

A pocket full of seeds to carry dandelion wishes.

Godspeed Christians.

# About the Author

Gene is the kind of man who comes home to say:
"My tire went flat today, but I was already at work – *isn't that great!?*"

He is the king of silver-linings.
He looks for the beauty in a situation. He looks for the beauty in people.

Sometimes he comes home with a story of a bank teller he saw that day;
other days he shares an exchange from someone in the grocery store.

And for a time…
Gene came home with stories of his time spent working for the man
running to become:
The President of the United States of America.

He coined a phrase:
*"Greatness is seldom seen in close proximity."*

He maintains this belief while searching for it in others. It suits him.

****

Gene Ho was born in Brooklyn and raised in Kings Park, New York.
He spoke Chinese as his first language and learned a great appreciation and love for America.

At 18, Gene relocated to Myrtle Beach, South Carolina to attend Coastal Carolina University. He began his career as a freelance writer for a local newspaper before taking on photography.
At age 23, he started his business as a professional photographer.

During this time, Gene grew his photography studio nationwide.
His staff photographed weddings "coast to coast" and internationally.
He is a requested speaker and has given photography seminars to thousands of professional photographers from Las Vegas to New York. He has also photographed some of the nation's top celebrities in politics, sports and the arts.

Gene is the father of four unique and amazing young people.
In a promise to God, Gene pledged to support a charity involving children pending the birth of our first son.
He chose Victory Junction.
To this day, Gene has been a loud and faithful advocate of this charity.
His Public Service Announcement for Victory Junction has appeared nationwide.

Gene takes to the world in his eccentric shoes and larger than life personality,
but few know the real man.
He is a goofy homebody who loves country music and oysters.
He's far from perfect, but the life we've built together is perfect for us.

I am as proud that he's mine as I am to be his.

- Nadean Bruehlman Ho

Printed in the United States
By Bookmasters